wandering mind books, berkeley california

hustlers grotto

three novellas

yayoi kusama

translated by ralph f. mccarthy

afterword by alexandra munroe

This is a work of fiction. Any resemblance to persons living or dead is purely coincidental.

English translation copyright © 1997 by Ralph F. McCarthy. All rights reserved. Printed in the United States of America. No part of this book may be used or reproduced in any manner whatsoever without written permission, except in the case of brief quotations embodied in critical articles and reviews. For information write to Wandering Mind Books, 1324 Peralta Avenue, Berkeley, CA 94702.

"The Hustlers Grotto of Christopher Street" was originally published in Japan as *Kurisutofā danshōkutsu* (Tokyo: Kadokawa Shoten, 1983) and re-issued as an anthology in 1989 by Jiritsu Shobō, Tokyo.

"Foxgloves of Central Park" was originally published as *Sentoraru pāku no jigitarisu* (Tokyo: Jiritsu Shobō, 1992).

"Death Smell Acacia" was originally published in Japanese as *Shishū akashia* in *Yasei jidai* magazine in 1984 and re-issued in the anthology *Kurisutofā danshōkutsu* (Tokyo: Jiritsu Shobō, 1989).

Cover art: *Sex Obsession* by Yayoi Kusama, 1992, acrylic on canvas, 76 $^{3}/_{8}$ in. x 153 $^{3}/_{8}$ in. (3 panels). Courtesy of Robert Miller Gallery, New York.

Back cover art: Photo-montage portrait of Yayoi Kusama by Eikoh Hosoe, 1964. Courtesy of Yayoi Kusama, Tokyo.

Special thanks to: Ryu Murakami, Alexandra Munroe, Leza Lowitz, Josh Cohen, the Café Muse, and Nina, Edith and Milton. —RFM

Design by Edith Zolotow.
Production by Gale Hengesch.
Printed by West Coast Print Center, Berkeley, California.
Published by Wandering Mind Books, Berkeley, California.

First edition, 1998

ISBN 0-9653304-2-7

Table of Contents

The Hustlers Grotto of Christopher Street   9

Foxgloves of Central Park   69

Death Smell Acacia   129

Afterword by Alexandra Munroe   159

the hustlers

grotto of

christopher street

The lion sculpture with its grinning discolored purple face glared down at the steps. Grinning or glaring? The way its expression seemed to change from one moment to the next, it was impossible to judge the animal's mood as you passed below.

    Yanni, looking up at the lion from outside the gay bar GEEZE on the corner of Christopher Street, noticed that the paint on the porch ceiling had discolored as well, to an ashen gray, and the apartment building itself seemed about to collapse. A flash of light from a window overlooking the porch pierced her eyes. Apparently he had the strobe light on, in the middle of the afternoon. Blinds covered the window, but each powerful blast of the strobe leaked out in thin stripes. Certain that Henry was in there, enveloped in that light, Yanni clattered up the steps. Pushing the front door open with her foot, she gave the white knob on the door to his room a hard twist. It didn't give. "Henry!" she shouted several times before the door suddenly swung open. From beyond the flaking cerulean blue paint wafted a wave of sickening sweat-and-urine-scented air. A shadow wriggled amid the fetid heat and sat up on wrinkled gray bed sheets.

After each flash of the strobe light Henry's bird's-nest Afro melted into the deep purple darkness. When a split second later the light flashed again his body was floating there in the room like a ghost swimming through space; the outline of his nude figure was stamped repeatedly on the air as he moved. The silhouette emblazoned on Yanni's retina slid from the sheets and stood up irritably.

The younger of Henry's two older brothers, Roy, was a proof printer at a woodcut studio. He lived nearby, on West 4th Street. Two days before, Henry had broken in Roy's door with a claw hammer and ransacked his apartment. The things he managed to make off with had netted a mere thirty dollars. "My brother, he's awful hard up these days," Henry complained, shaking his head. "Unless he hid all his money when I kept hittin' up on him." He'd converted the thirty dollars into white powder earlier that day.

He opened the drawer on the dilapidated desk next to his bed, extracted a small paper packet, poured the heroin out on the palm of his hand, and grumbled to Yanni. He'd bought this shit from Richard the dealer, it was cut with something, not even fifty percent pure, he wasn't going to buy from that bastard any more. Fuming, he sat back down on the bed, crossed his legs Indian style, and began to entreat Yanni for work, his eyes wide and pleading.

"If you got any johns for me, I want you to fix me up right away. I need a little advance. Can you get me a hundred dollars or so by about ten o'clock tonight?"

Beads of sweat exuded from Henry's obsidian skin and dripped down on sheets that hadn't been washed since he'd bought them two years before. The stained fabric clinging to his thighs absorbed the hot fluid drop by drop. His kinky Afro stuck out in every direction, as if he'd been struck by lightning. Once again that indescribable smell wafted through the room and filled Yanni's nostrils, nearly causing her to gag.

"Can I have a glass of water?" she managed to say as she collected her thoughts. Which if any of her better customers could she get hold of on the spur of the moment? It was already late afternoon. Most of the johns she knew had undoubtedly found themselves a nice babyfaced chicken by now and were setting out on their dates for the evening.

"You want to score tonight?" she muttered, looking at her watch.

"Thirty bucks worth of junk won't last me three days. Yeah, I wanna work, if you can think of anybody. I'd be happy with some old guy, 'long as he's rich. What I need most right now is money."

The flickering light only served to intensify the probing haggard eyes of the black junkweary panther before her.

A few years ago, as a student at NYU, Henry had started out merely snorting heroin occasionally. But as the days passed, he'd slipped deeper into the abyss of addiction, skin-popping and finally mainlining the stuff. Since the year before, he'd been shooting up with greater and greater frequency and having a hard time supporting his habit. He'd hardly eaten anything at all for the past three days. With the ebbing of his appetite and sex drive, he'd begun to concentrate only on getting by one day at a time. Two months ago, in the middle of the night, he'd smashed the show window of a jewelry store on 8th Street in the Village and stolen a brooch and a ring, which he'd immediately sold to a fence. The police tracked him down, and a detective from the NYPD arrested him. His oldest brother, who ran a delicatessen in the Bronx, had bailed him out just a week earlier.

Yanni reached out with her right hand to open the blinds and let some light into the small squalid room. A sparkling crimson lake sunset streaked with egg-yolk yellow filled the window as if it were painted on the glass. One corner of the glass was broken, leaving a triangular opening.

An evening breeze from the Hudson River, having weaved through the masts of foreign ships moored at the piers, converged on the three-cornered hole in Henry's window.

The air in the room seemed to shift suddenly. Henry stood up. He turned on the faucet in the corner sink and stooped to let the warm water run over his head. The water pipes on the roof, exposed all day to the sun, were still hot. Water sprayed over the tiny kitchenette and caught the light of sunset through the window, creating a madder-red arc that instantly resolved into a rainbow.

Yanni took from her pocket a small red dog-eared address book. As she leafed through the list of clients the faces of two or three of her more reliable patrons flashed through her mind.

Retrieving the black telephone from beneath the bed, she sat down and began making calls. Not likely to have much luck tonight, she thought. It was too late in the day, for one thing. Six o'clock Saturday evening. Sunlight still remained in the glowing color-drenched clouds, but by this time all her gay gentlemen would have surely found partners and disappeared into the discos, parks, restaurants, and coffee shops. The elderly lawyer Styne wasn't home. Next she called Mr. Levin, who owned a food wholesaling company on 8th Street and collected pop art. The maid said he'd gone to see the Broadway musical "Elephant!" Yanni thanked her and hung up.

At that moment someone stopped outside the door to Henry's room. Henry tensed visibly. A customer? The police? A few days before, the cops had raided the building in connection with a heroin and cocaine ring. A youth living upstairs from Henry had been the cause of it all. Billy, who'd been peddling drugs for the mob since he'd moved to New York, had got himself busted, and since then the police had been picking up one resident of the building after another. These were trying times.

Perhaps five minutes had passed before the person outside the door moved on and they heard footsteps ascending the staircase. Breathing a sigh of relief, both of them let their eyes rest on that slab of mackerel sky visible through the broken window. Snagged in a wire mesh fence on the roof of the building facing them were two or three small downy feathers. A little bird darted lightly through an opening in the mesh and out into the sky.

The evening breeze chased after it.

In a while the uncanny red afterglow faded from the edges of clouds and the sunset colors grew quietly dimmer. The little bird who'd left her feathers in the wire mesh returned and perched in one of the openings. The mesh was moist with liquid that dripped from between the bird's soft breast feathers. The warm drops glistened in the sunlight still shining through gaps in the clouds and quickly evaporated. A male bird, spotting his companion, swooped down from the sky.

The expression on Henry's face grew ever more distraught as he watched the birds at play.

Lying low all day deep in the interiors of buildings, the hustlers begin to awaken phoenix-like from their deathly slumber and prepare for night. Transforming themselves with apparel designed to lure their male prey. By the time the sky is painted in lovely sunset colors, the rectums of all are filled to capacity.

Facing a johnless night, Henry's nerves were on edge. The sun was sinking mercilessly behind the New Jersey skyline.

Yanni managed to contact a certain rectally oriented gentleman on the final page of her client list. To have reached him by telephone at this time of day was nothing short of miraculous. His name was Robert Greenberg. Mr. Greenberg had returned late that afternoon from the beach, and after a cold shower was relaxing on his black velvet sofa.

Though Yanni was pressing him to hurry, Henry bent over the kitchenette sink before setting out from the hustlers grotto on Christopher Street. With the water that spurted from the faucet he swept away the musky black odor that cloaked his body. Over his refreshed skin a red T-shirt with the face of Malcolm X embossed on the front in black, and faded blue jeans. He'd stolen them both from the second floor of Klein's in Union Square East the previous year.

It was getting harder and harder to shoplift at department stores these days, what with store detectives disguised as customers roaming the aisles. Nor were department stores alone in this regard. Even neighborhood boutiques were making things difficult. Attached to hems and seams of T-shirts and dresses were small inconspicuous plastic tags, and when the shoplifter tried nonchalantly to walk out the door a buzzer in the ceiling would let out a heartless wail.

    The downtown boys and girls complained bitterly: it was getting tough to get by in this world. Since the Vietnam war even New York had gone to hell. For the kids downtown, the only way left to make a few quick bucks was to turn to hustling. No need for capital. All you needed was what you were born with: the equipment between your legs and the orifice behind you. It was a business anyone could break into anytime, anywhere.

    Since settling in the big city at the age of seventeen, having arrived from New Orleans with his two elder brothers, Henry'd earned enough money hustling to put himself through college. He'd been living quite well, in fact, until he began to dabble in heroin.

    It was, of course, junk that had so definitively messed up his life since graduation. While still studying economics at NYU he'd fallen in with a group of users in the law department and soon needed to make more money than hustling alone could provide. At last he'd got so hard up that he tried his hand at being a jewel thief. Renting his anus to chicken hawks simply wasn't enough to cover his drug expenses.

Henry and Yanni walked along the edge of the Hudson River.

Beyond the Hudson, swathed in shadows now that the sun had gone down, was the New Jersey skyline. The deep, swollen waters of the river flowed silently, dividing Manhattan from the craggy shore of New Jersey as it made its way to the harbor to mix with the ocean tides. The great river had a benevolence and magnanimity about it that offered succor to travelers from around the world, though up close you could see it was full of trash and stagnant with sewage and filth brought downstream by the current. Nonetheless, each wavelet shone pure and colorless in the dusk as it absorbed the lingering light that leaked through the clouds.

The two of them stopped in front of a restaurant facing the river.

The collar of Robert Greenberg's shirt, blue with white checks, peeked out from his linen jacket, setting off his suntanned face and giving him a calculated older-but-still-sexy look.

Seeing Yanni enter from the darkening street and pause at the waiting area, he stood up and approached her. It was dinner time, and the Italian restaurant Cactus was packed.

He glanced at Henry behind her.

"That was quick, lucky I happened to be home this evening, I was thinking about catching a movie in Times Square, five minutes later and you'd have missed me."

He said all this in one breath, perspiration beading his forehead.

They sat at his table. The surface of the Hudson River was dark now, having turned off its play of reflections in preparation for the approaching festival of night. The waiter brought a plate of Italian salad, and when he left, Greenberg looked up at Yanni.

"So this is the young man? Hm? Henry? He has beautiful eyes."

Yanni knew it wasn't just flattery. Henry really was beautiful. His skin was extraordinarily dark, even for a black person. The whites of his large eyes dazzlingly bright in contrast. The tight curls of his raven hair. Greenberg studied him, obviously captivated. By the time they'd all finished dessert, Yanni had begun to negotiate a price.

"From now till tomorrow morning, Mr. Greenberg. How does three hundred dollars sound?"

Greenberg was somewhat taken aback.

"That's a bit expensive, isn't it? I was planning on something more along the lines of a hundred and fifty, at the most. Can't you come down a little? I'll gladly date him on a regular basis if the price is right."

"How about this, then?" said Yanni. "Three full days and nights for five hundred."

Greenberg thought for a moment, then spoke as if he'd hit upon a brilliant solution: six hundred dollars for a week with Henry at his summer house in New Jersey.

Now it was Yanni's turn to consider. Not bad, she thought. Nor was Henry likely to have any objections. A week wasn't so long—it would be over before he knew it. Six hundred bucks all at once would buy him a bit of breathing space and make even seven days with this boring old fellow bearable.

The deal was struck. Henry agreed to go to New Jersey with Greenberg.

Greenberg rose, paid for their dinner, and showed Henry to his white Porsche parked in front of the restaurant.

As they walked out, he handed Yanni the six hundred dollars. She quickly counted the money at the curb, then stuffed the roll of bills into her purse. She didn't give Henry so much as a dollar. She knew if she settled with him then and there he'd be gone. She'd made that mistake twice last year.

After leaving Henry in Greenberg's hands, Yanni returned to her apartment on Christopher Street, a few blocks from Washington Square. The hot day had ended. She'd found Henry a customer and negotiated a deal, but Henry, undergoing withdrawal, might botch things yet. She was beginning to realize just how long a week was. But Greenberg had seemed quite enamored. There was an eighty or ninety percent chance they'd get on well. Wasn't there? The truth is that she was more than a little anxious about it all.

Greenberg, with Henry beside him, was soaring seventy miles an hour up the highway that ran along the Hudson. A gaily illuminated passenger ship out of Rotterdam was docked at the pier, side by side with freighters that plied the European routes. Beyond them lay the dark river.

The wedge of the Porsche sliced through the summer heat and carried them in a cool breeze to the George Washington Bridge.

Below the bridge a ship was plowing upstream from New York Bay. Slowly. Compared to the Porsche it seemed to be standing still. As the wind slashed through the bridge's alternating strips of darkness and illumination, the black tree-covered palisades of New Jersey began to loom up before them. The car sped on, leaving the bridge behind, and at that moment they noticed for the first time the stars twinkling in the sky. Neither of them spoke.

They turned at the intersection commonly known as Saint Neurosis and flew past James Elementary School, near the stop for the Orangeburg bus. Greenberg's summer house was situated in a dark and silent grove of beeches. The Porsche, disrupting the dark serenity of the private driveway, pulled up before the front porch and came to a halt.

Greenberg switched on the lamp over the entrance. The vivid green of the lawn flared up in the light. The two of them, delivered from the chasm of crowded chaotic New York and its feverish pace of life, drew the spirit of night into their lungs and exchanged a passionate kiss there beneath the porch light. The last rays of the blazing sun still lingered in the treetops. But on the grass-covered ground the evening dew was already emerging, preparing to spread its morning veil.

Greenberg drew Henry out of the nocturnal forest air and in through the front door. With the door at his back he once again sucked hungrily at Henry's lips.

With this second kiss, Henry promptly began to find Greenberg offensive. The first had been a natural part of his job, but he'd intentionally made it seem passionate because he believed the man could be a valuable customer for him in the future. It annoyed him to be kissed twice like that without even getting a chance to rest, weary as he was, having just driven all the way from New York. But his professionalism as a hustler wouldn't permit any overt show of anger. Yanni was constantly warning him about that.

It was not because he liked the work that Henry'd become a hustler. The truth is he found it much easier to have affairs with women. The women he knew were kind to him; they prepared his meals, did his laundry, and generally looked after him as a mother would for a child. His queer customers, on the other hand, provided him with financial support but did nothing for his peace of mind.

Henry had become a hustler at eighteen. At first the pain—and the disgust that bordered on loathing—of having a thick cock penetrate his anus, was something he thought it would be impossible to forget until the day he died. He'd also suffered horribly from hemorrhoids. His second elder brother, Roy the printer, had often lectured him.

"You be doin' shit like that, you gonna get cancer of the rectum. When God gave you your asshole, he only meant for you to use it to shit with, man. Even you use the money for college, you ain't gonna get no respect from me. I may not look like much to you, but I make a respectable living as a proof printer. How'm I supposed to hold my head up high walkin' down Broadway when my little brother's a male hustler? C'mon, Henry, you quit this fag business, that's all I ask."

But Henry was always ready with an answer.

"Roy, look at the art world in New York. To get ahead, artists be sleepin' with the art collectors or the museum directors they makin' deals with. Pop artists like Jerome Michaelson or Larry Sanders, say, they both ex-hustlers who made it big. Theater world the same, overflowin' with homo actors and dancers. Hairdressers, even, they style the hair of some ballet dancer from Europe, they throw in a little sex. And get tipped for it, of course. So there's nothin' wrong with me rentin' my body to grown-up faggots. I don't plan to be doin' this my whole life, y'know. It's just a fast and sure way to get my hands on some money."

The one who'd set him up as a hustler was Yanni, who in those days was a student in the philosophy department of Columbia University. She chose and refined her stock in trade—her boys, that is—from among her acquaintances at NYU, Columbia, Cornell, and other schools. She always had close to twenty boys at her command. The students were rented out to the homosexuals of New York through the Paranoiac Club, a secret organization Yanni managed. She'd started with some twenty members, but that number grew as she gathered students who'd failed to get jobs as dishwashers and what have you, students who were hard pressed to pay tuition and living expenses. Most of these boys lived around Christopher Street, near the Hudson River, an area well known as a hunting ground for homosexual gents from uptown.

Christopher Street was a chaotic mob-infested neighborhood fanning out from the wharves for foreign ships. It was renowned as a haunt for buyers of hashish, marijuana, and narcotics such as heroin and cocaine smuggled in from Marseilles and Spain. When foreign seamen sold drugs, it was always in the area surrounding Christopher Street. The police insinuated themselves into this neighborhood, offering the drug brokers protection in exchange for bribes. The drugs generally went from the foreign ships to Mafia brokers to small-time dealers, then to the police who confiscated them in busts and sold them back to the brokers—a cyclical process that resulted in ever-increasing profits.

In the midst of protests over police collaboration in the drug trade, the opening of a sex toys shop by mob kingpin "Cobra" Doyle caused a lot of controversy. As

21

one of the first public sex businesses, the shop was a topic of nighttime gossip throughout New York. It hadn't taken long for Robert Greenberg, real estate man, to make his way to this shop and arrange through Boyle an introduction to Yanni. Yanni had taken Mr. Greenberg around to several different apartment buildings on Christopher Street, introducing him to young male students. In the course of a week she might place two or three boys in his hands, for which she received one-third of the fee as commission.

 She frequently walked around the campus of Columbia University when classes were done, killing time and speaking to every charming student she met. They always resisted at first, saying they couldn't possibly do such a thing and acting as if their pride had been wounded. All she had to do, however, was flash the cash they'd receive in advance, and most of them would show up on Christopher Street at the appointed hour. They'd wait in a coffee shop to meet the customer and set out on a date that very night. But once they were securely on this road, what always awaited them next was the quagmire of drugs.

 In terms of income, such jobs as washing dishes at a restaurant or selling dresses during the evening hours or being a night watchman at a factory simply couldn't compare. It was almost a given that these boys would get involved with drugs. Nor were students the only ones to be tempted. All young people were equally hungry for food and money. Like starving dogs, they could eat and eat and never be satisfied. In the great metropolis of youth, money was truly no more than scraps of paper. Especially money earned with the anus. Such dollars were like old pages of the *New York Times* being blown and scattered by the wind down the gutters of 14th Street. Just as news is printed on paper only to be read and discarded, money had no meaning or value to these kids except as something to be thrown away. In a great city like New York, the psychic significance of material objects was a vague and ambiguous quantity. Money and goods weren't things you earned by working. They were things you stole. Stuff was just there for the taking.

Henry was in the kitchen downstairs brewing a pot of coffee and pouring it into two cups when Mr. Greenberg called for him to come to the bedroom on the second floor. As Henry ambled in, Greenberg said:
  "Call me Robert. Or better yet, Bob."
  Judging from this attempt at familiarity, Greenberg obviously thought of them as lovers already. This though they'd met only hours earlier. Or was he simply saying that, though there was no telling what the night might bring, at least they could be on a first-name basis? Bob placed the two coffee cups on the table beside the bed and took a sip. Then he gently reached over and turned out the light. A moth flew in through the dark window and landed in Henry's coffee, scattering tiny scales—silver dust that fell from its wings as it scraped them on the white porcelain rim of the cup. For a moment the surface of the coffee turned from brown to a vivid silver. They thought it was starlight streaming in through a corner of the window. Surely that was what it had been—a silver falling star. It was as if the star had collided with their four pupils and disintegrated. Lured into the atmosphere by

earth's gravity, it had crashed, sprinkling its powdery silver dust in the men's eyes before vaporizing. At that moment the window frame seemed to be filled once again with the green of the forest trees that had melted into the dark. When the silhouettes of the two men, embedded in the square green-dyed darkness of the frame, flickered like the hesitant love-call of man to man, Bob murmured this question:

"Henry, are you bi? I mean, do you also go with women?"

Henry was at a loss for an answer. He could scarcely admit he had a physical relationship with Yanni, whom they'd been with just a short while before. Jaw clenched, he leaned quietly forward. As his face neared the silent window he could see, glittering in the distance like jewels, the skyscrapers, concert halls, and theaters that make up the skyline of New York City, a battleship floating in midair.

That enormous stone ship, encompassing the light of countless lamps, made no forward progress whatsoever. Afloat far beyond the pitch dark forest, it seemed to stir not an inch. Henry grew gradually more bewitched by this ship of stone that shone and sparkled beyond the dark sea of trees. In that moment, for the first time, he felt a brief liberation from the unpleasant drudgery of the evening's date.

Whenever he was out of junk and walking the streets of New York in the daytime, the rectangular windows of the buildings would appear to him as dollar bills, or ten dollar bills, causing his head to swim. And gazing disconsolately up at the Empire State Building from Times Square, he couldn't help but see it as a phallus. This when there were no customers and he was without work. As he roamed the streets looking for marks his impatience would turn to anger which he'd direct at the great building, glaring up at it. But the building would merely gaze back down at him, still as a rock, as white clouds shrouded the tip of the tower and then passed on. That looming symbol of manhood would fill Henry with self-loathing. At times like these his eyes would begin to sting and he would find himself unable to open them as he fell captive to an incapacitating dizziness.

Now that very Empire State Building, beyond the mighty Hudson, bejeweled the night sky with hundreds of lights, doing its best to help lift him from his depression.

As the summer heat that had beat down upon the ground all day slowly escaped from the forest one leaf at a time to be replaced by the cool of evening, would love steal into the gap between the two men? Henry's heart used his eyes to weave through the starlight; it would take time for him to loosen up enough to be open to sex.

Bob was in high spirits at the prospect of spending a week's vacation with this beautiful young black man. Henry, on the other hand, felt the six hundred dollar copulation fee weighing heavily upon him, triggering an almost lunatic fury at times, though the next moment he'd forget himself once again, entranced by the shapes of the branches in the nightdark forest. The sky was enchased with diamonds, as if it were raining stars. He would have liked to pull all of those seven-night-six-hundred-dollar stars down from the sky and flee back to Manhattan. This impulse gradually escalated into an intense anger focused on Yanni.

When he thought about being shut up in this summer house for seven days without being able to return to New York, he was overwhelmed with remorse at not having brought a needle and junk.

Too late now, of course, but it was agonizing to think of himself alone with this older man in the deserted woods of New Jersey, and the fact that it was for money was little consolation. Henry wanted to go back to New York. If this were an ordinary sex-trade transaction, he'd receive so much per hour and afterwards be free. After jobs like that he could return to his apartment on Christopher Street and crash for as long as he liked. Working three days a week or so was just right. When your business was done you could go watch kids play baseball in Central Park or whatever. But now, seduced by the six hundred dollars, he'd come all the way to New Jersey to be a kept man. Being a sex slave in the woods at night was an unbearably gloomy proposition. In the darkness of the room the expression on Henry's face grew ever grimmer.

Relying on the dim light of the window, Bob groped for the desk drawer, removed a cigarette case, and offered Henry a smoke.

As the two red points of light glowed in the darkness and a purple fragrance wafted through the room, a breeze caressing the forest skyline stirred a whisper of leaves in the great oaks of the garden. The shadows of the trees transformed into gigantic phalluses that intimidated the forest and stood blocking Henry's path. At the same time the shadows grew even emptier in their blackness. Cigarette smoke wafted out through the window and cloaked the trees in a thin purple curtain. The shadows of the two bodies, too, began to wriggle and swim in the curtain of smoke. At some point they'd discarded all their clothing. Soon, with the rubbing and pressing of white flesh against black, a maniacal rage boiled up inside Henry, and he suddenly rose to his feet on the bed and began to shout.

"I'm only here because I want the money! You prob'ly really believe I'm a homo just 'cause Yanni told you I am. But every time I have sex with a man I end up wantin' to bash his fuckin' brains in! Goddamn it! Buyin' my ass for a week for a lousy six hundred bucks! You fuckin' Jewish prick!"

No sooner had he finished shouting these words, however, than he plopped back down, deflated, as if he'd suddenly remembered something.

Each of Yanni's boys had his own peculiarities. But Henry in particular was forever causing her grief. What greater misfortune than that the brightest star in her club, a youth like the biblical David incarnate, should have an aversion to sodomy? Even the fairest roses have thorns.

"I'm sorry, darlin'. My nerves are kind of on edge right now. Don't mind what I just said. Starting tonight, I'll spend a whole week in bed with you, I swear to God. I'm sorry I shouted."

Still taken aback, Bob said, "So you just ... It's only for money that you do this? That's unusual. Most boys, even if they feel that way at first, end up really liking men once they've become this deeply involved ..."

This awkwardness too eventually melted into the darkness along with the purple smoke, and joined the sweat and the sweetsour odor of bodies in greeting the onset of night.

The two bodies floated and bobbed, throbbing as they pressed and joined together in a soft film of sweat. Henry's strawberry-colored lips, embedded in the black field of his face, were planted on Bob's white crotch. Bob let out a faint groan when the white teeth inside the strawberry gently nibbled his white banana.

"Do you really ... I mean, you said you don't like men, but ... Do you really dislike me?" Bob asked between gasps.

You at least love my body, don't you, is what Henry imagined Bob was trying to say, and he was waiting for him to continue. Waiting because with his answer to the next question, he intended to demolish any hope Bob might have left. But Bob surprised him.

"I thank God for letting me meet a beautiful young man like you tonight," he said. "It's enough to make me forget my love for all the other young men I've met in my life. Wait and see: you're going to learn to love men—or, rather, me. I'm going to make you love me. If you can be satisfied with my love, I'm prepared to take responsibility for your livelihood—to ensure that you lack nothing each month. I'll talk it over with your boss—with Yanni—if you like. What do you think?"

Henry was stunned. He would never have dreamed that this last bit, about ensuring his livelihood, would issue from Bob's lips so soon, and so unequivocally. It left him flustered. The words he'd been readying in his heart, the words with which he'd planned to plunge Bob into the depths of despair, were buried now beneath his confusion.

It was true that Henry possessed a dazzling beauty,

like an antelope carved from black diamonds. His flashing gaze, which flickered with the urgent need for junk, seemed to the unknowing Bob to bespeak a lovely melancholy, like sparkling drops that fall from the stars as they blink, and aroused in him a burning desire not even a rainstorm of kisses could quench.

Having squandered his youth in affairs with any number of men, Bob was inwardly appalled at how his body lost vigor and beauty each day as old age drew near.

It was like a brush fire burning atop a hill at sunset, the flames gradually spreading over a field of platinum grass. The patch of dry grass at his feet grew smaller and smaller as the sun sank beneath the horizon behind him, leaving him all alone with his fears. During the lonely days he spent on the sofa in his house in Manhattan, thoughts of his ex-wife and son in faraway Los Angeles never so much as crossed his mind. They, after all, lived in a totally different world.

A nuisance of wombs flying directly in the face of a man whose forehead drips greasy sweat. At his feet, the quiet glasslike surface of a pure and limpid lake. He wants to gaze at his own loveliness in that pale silver water. The lake bottom is carpeted with narcissus petals. That mysterious mirror never tires of swallowing lovely young men. The lake is starving, a victim of its own rapacious appetite for Adonises. Love and Beauty, wandering these hills, are forever drawn to it. Men peer into the water only to have their souls pulled under and drowned. The banks of the lake maintain a grim solemnity that keeps women away. The desire to draw near the waters. The manhunters, like Bob, use it to lure all their boys. The youths, in need of cash, appear at the lake one after the other. For a certain amount of money, enough to keep them in drugs for the day, they flock to its shores.

In the hustlers grotto of Christopher Street the beautiful Davids that inhabit the rows of apartment buildings keep their rooms dark in the daytime, closing their blinds against the sun and devouring sleep. But when night arrives, whispers of love rekindle the flame of fleshly desire by falling to earth with the stars and prowling beside the waveless lake of Narcissus. During such days as these, the pale young narcissus buds have no time for warming to women. The youths spend all the daylight hours exposed to the scorching landlocked sun, searching for marks among the sightseers. They loiter on Washington Square or get picked up on Christopher Street by gay foreign seamen who've come from the piers to look for fun in Manhattan.

Wealthy middle-aged or elderly homosexual gentlemen like Bob were everywhere. That it had been difficult recently for Henry and other chickens to find johns was due to the fact that young would-be hustlers from all over America—boys for whom money was secondary to the desire for adventure—had been flocking to Manhattan, particularly downtown. All of them were competitors as far as Henry was concerned. As were the other residents of Henry's five-story brick apartment building, all of whom—with the exception of Billy, who made a living dealing drugs—were also involved in male prostitution. Most of them just got by from day to day. They financed one another, borrowing and lending money, and sometimes even shared their food. On rainy days, business on the street corners could turn as bleak as the weather. At times like that it was best to call Yanni's organization, the Paranoiac Club, and have her find you a client. Yanni earned her commission simply by phoning her regular customers and sending them boys. It was amusing to her how easily the money came in. All she needed was a telephone. Mr. Greenberg was an official member of her clandestine organization. He'd met dozens of homosexual boys and young men through this club.

But never, he thought as he caressed Henry's body, had he met a boy as beautiful and captivating as this.

The chickens Bob had had sex with so far—even those who weren't necessarily gay—would invariably greet their client with a face that suggested they considered this path, the path of manly love, the highest form of art. That was part of the ABCs of hustling—or, rather, of prostitution in general.

In spite of which, the relatively unsubmissive Henry earned more than most. He may have been the top moneymaker of all, in fact.

But the money he earned was no sooner in his hands that it was gone. It was almost like magic, the way he made it disappear.

Henry was, yes, an insatiable soul, a vagabond of the night who roamed the pleasure quarters seeking dissipation and oblivion. He used money to ransom food and drugs, and in order to obtain that money he begrudgingly sold his flesh and his anus. The fact that business on the corners was so affected by the weather put him on the same level as a street performer.

But no matter how much junk he injected, it was never enough. His appetite and sex drive decreased daily, in inverse proportion to his growing need, and he was becoming more and more enervated. To have to work the sex trade each day disgusted him, especially now that the drugs had eaten away at his libido.

Far above the roof over the bed where he lay in the dark tonight with Bob, billions of stars twinkled away as if nothing extraordinary were going on, from time to time dragging tails of light across farflung fields to crash into the earth. The fragments of stars that rained on Henry's head were not enough to soothe his young but desolate heart. Not even the rustling of the billion leaves in the vast black New Jersey forest had the power to ease his pain.

Bob's embrace grew even more passionate. His passion was as far from Henry's disgust as Heaven is from Earth, and the distance between them grew with each creak of the bedsprings.

The two bodies became a single silhouette, writhing in anticipation of the diversions that lay ahead. The deeper into melancholy this beautifully built young black man sank, the more Bob, who was about to begin a rapid descent down the mountain of aging flesh, burned with the flame of infinite longing for youth. This red-roofed room surrounded by silent woods was no longer the temporary abode of love but of what had transformed, with one stroke, into a vexing duel of souls. By now, in Henry's head, it was as if the earth had exploded. One moment of delusion followed another. A spark shot out of his brain and bounced off the ground; a falling star became a pale glint of light as it made its way down. Reversing its course now, it ascended toward the heavens at an impossible speed, faster even than the light of the stars. At that moment, Henry's soul shivered with solitude. It was not possible for Bob, with his passionate caresses and his heartfelt words of love, to steal the gray brooding loneliness from this young man's soul.

The game of love for hire, contracted for six hundred dollars on the flip side of that soul, was still in progress. The stage upon which this sex-for-money show was to be enacted had now, at last, caught fire. But all that was burning as yet was one end of a length of rope. It was going to be a long, long seven days.

Though Bob's fingers parted Henry's black pubic hair and gripped his penis gently, squeezing it from time to time, it remained hopelessly flaccid. No hot blood rushed to engorge the tip of Henry's slender and soft little member. A jellyfish floating limply in the dark, responding to Bob's love-call with only a clammy flopping from side to side. A line Henry's "boss" was forever reciting flitted through his mind: "As long as the customer's paying you, it's your duty to serve him." But exhaustion from the hot Manhattan summer and the self-loathing that gnawed at him always, along with his growing revulsion toward sex, made an erection out of the question. He had no choice, then, but to reposition himself and bury his black face in Bob's crotch to take that white appendage into his mouth once again. The repeated fellatio required a lot of endurance; it was enough to scorch his throat and cause his lips to swell. Bob's penis, engorging with blood, grew fatter even as it passed over Henry's tongue, retreating one moment only to obstinately close in again the next. How many dozens of times did that dark white rod slide back and forth across his tongue? It was there that it gradually transformed into a small living creature.

Tiring perhaps of this game, Bob at last guided his hotblooded little animal toward Henry's anus.

Henry's entire body stiffened with an unspeakable dread.

What expression does the white hunter wear with his antelope prey before him? Henry could only imagine a violent panting of breath.

It was dark enough in the room that the red tip of a cigarette stood out in bold relief. Until now, Bob's white penis had existed merely as a vague if hideous little clump of a creature in Henry's field of vision, but now it was unleashing its fiery passion on every part of his anatomy—his cock, his skin, his asshole, his lips ... For Henry, the one-sided attentions of this white goblin were nothing less than ludicrous. The chickenhawk was leaving no stone unturned in a relentless attack on his vital parts. But Henry's anus was too tightly closed. His anus alone was maintaining a mute resistance.

Finally Bob, half-resigned perhaps, once again reached in the dark for the desk drawer to take out his cigarettes, as if to pull himself together. The little red spot, swathed in purple smoke, glowed for a second time in the darkness, but even this spark of ignition was aimed at Henry's anus, a warning signal.

Since infancy, Henry had opened his anus each day to offer his feces to the world. But such offerings were shut up today behind a "forbidden door." The most fundamental rule in Yanni's "Primer of Hustling"—*Surrender your anus freely to the client to do with as he sees fit*—was of no use whatsoever to him now. His head and his body were locked away in separate rooms.

The man who's miserly to an absurd extreme. The man who can't stop washing his hands. The man who stands before a mirror checking and readjusting his hat dozens of times and still isn't satisfied. The man whose slovenliness is such that his room is littered with a year's worth of cigarette butts. The man who walks about town salvaging rubbish and who actually enjoys poking his nose in trashcans on the street. The man who shamelessly and unrelentingly demands a discount on even a carton of milk. The man who steals all sorts of things he has no use for, piles them in his room, and gets up in the middle of the night to inspect his treasures and smirk to himself. The man who keeps removing his savings passbook from a drawer and poring over it, though there's nothing very impressive about the sums inside. The man who's so obsessed with neatness that he isn't content to spend the entire day cleaning his spotless room, but must make a poster saying "CLEANLINESS FIRST," which he hangs on the wall and delights in studying. The man who's such an extreme egoist that he always insists on having his way, even when it makes no difference whatsoever, and as a result has failed to get ahead in the world. The man who wants others to bully him. The man who's afraid to put his money in the bank so keeps a jar of moldy bills in a hole he's dug beneath the floor and sits above it all day each day smoking cigarettes. The men who, by being overly eager to become independent, fail to achieve independence, lose hope, and commit suicide. These men have all been kept frantically busy throughout their lives as a consequence of the unnameable, ghostly air that wafts about the anus.

Lost in the anus's ghostly air of degradation and obsession, they are enticed away from the soul's freedom, to prowl surreptitiously behind the curtain surrounding prisoners of narcissism. Though they turn to the left or lean to the right, their nerves, forged within the framework of their hearts, are at the mercy of the storm of compulsion, and they find they cannot move. The anus's mucous membrane has a deep connection with sex and is the lofty goal of ambitious climbers of every description.

Throngs of men dominated by this their entire lives. Happiness, love—such things are for them no more than fantasies of having an anus at their beck and call. The dictionary of rectal business terms, terms to be whispered man to man, is underlined on every page, and no one in the entire world can say how much of this is a dream, how much a sickness, how much nervous excitement, and how much insanity. No one can say because we're restrained by propriety on the one hand and baldfaced lies on the other.

It would have been a tremendous problem had the police department found out about the Paranoiac Club. Not only was it a fullfledged prostitution ring, but drugs were involved. Yet at the same time, interestingly enough, any number of policemen would have loved to be members. There were, in fact, countless men from every conceivable profession who'd have liked to join clubs like this. As a result of which, American women had begun to protest vociferously, saying that the institution of marriage was doomed in this country and that the number of eligible bachelors was decreasing daily.

Recently the art critic Gregory Styrone and artists such as Ben Vonnegut, the action painter and leader of the New York school, had been renting a lecture hall at the university on Sundays to hold symposiums on art, literature, philosophy, and so on, gathering as many as five hundred students and raising funds by charging admission at the door. Calling them symposiums on culture was deceptive, however, considering the actual topics of discussion: the homosexuality of such towering figures in art history as Leonardo da Vinci, or how da Vinci's *Mona Lisa* was related to his interest in men, or how André Gide ... and so on. They would address these issues in all seriousness, twisting their goatees and dripping with sweat, for hours at a time. One after another they would step to the microphone on the podium and hold forth on topics of a pederastic nature. Even the president of the university was rumored to be queer.

Neither Henry nor any of his peers had ever attended a meeting of this sort. The members of the cultural gay revolution and the boys involved in the chicken trade downtown were, obviously, of different stripes. The youths from the hustlers grotto of Christopher Street kept things businesslike. They were aware that they'd never be able to legitimize what they did by carrying on about art. Because of the nature of trading money for sex, each day was individually colored by the situations it presented; everything was as transient as clouds floating by in the sky. The boys in Yanni's club were sold casually, as if they were cakes wrapped in pretty paper and tied with ribbons. They were not interested, therefore, in talking rot about homosexual art or how some artist like da Vinci, hundreds of years after his death, did this or that for the homosexuals of today. For them it was take the money, here's my asshole, see you later. This way was more New York—and more now. Some even saw themselves as being on the cutting edge of rationalism.

But Henry was sullen in his beauty tonight, a forbidding rose whose thorns drew blood with every touch.

Bob's white penis was once again stealthily creeping toward Henry's angry forbidden door. Like a small creature peering inside a hole before entering. At length, somewhat frustrated, Bob whispered:

"Henry, don't you like me?"

The question struck Henry as absurd. A sexual pervert and a dealer in perverted sex who pretended to be perverted lay one atop the other in bed, probing each other's hearts, negotiating over an anal cavity. The moth that had bumped its wings against the rim of the cup and scattered its scales was now sinking in a sea of coffee, its entire body saturated with caffeine. Its internal organs soaked brown, the moth was gasping in its final agony.

Henry suddenly and inexplicably sat up, took the cup from the table, and drank what remained of the coffee.

His tongue was sticky from Bob's body fluids and coated with a cloying, sour smell. The silver scales in the coffee slid over the surface of his tongue, which was so chafed from sucking Bob's member that it seemed to have lost the ability to taste. But though his tongue turned silver, the odor of body fluids could not be erased.

The silver coffee, which sparkled even in the night, dyed Henry's insides silver too. As his intestines changed color with the scales that had spilled from the moth's wings, Bob drew near once more. No doubt the interior of the forbidden door was now silver as well.

Henry's obsidian skin, the same color as the darkness into which his outline had melted. When his lips parted, it was like a petunia popping open in black space. And his teeth, white as only the teeth of blacks can be, and the whites of his eyes, glowing savagely in the night like the gaze of an animal lurking in the shadows of leaves, waiting for prey.

The subtler details of Bob's facial expression were lost in the dark, but his body was a large and looming white mass of meat. He was focused on Henry's anus and growing more forceful as he gradually began his assault on the black crevice.

The prey was paralyzed now, defenseless before the hunter. A black lump of yin and a white lump of yang, as different at heart as the moon and sun, stood facing one another. Perspiration alone fell impartially from the skin of each, dripping on to the mattress, which grew more ponderous with every drop. A mosquito buzzed blindly in through the window.

At precisely that moment, Yanni was in her apartment in downtown Manhattan watching a movie on television. She'd been glued to it for two hours now. Only during the short commercial breaks had she gone to the kitchen to pour coffee or visited the bathroom.

She was thinking about Henry: *He won't be back in Manhattan for seven days. Which means he won't be showing up here either.*

The movie on TV is about a black prostitute in the slums of Chicago who murders someone for drugs. In a valley between the skyscrapers, with her hair in wild disarray and the setting sun behind her, the blood-splattered whore shrinks back as her eyes fill the screen, glistening with tears. The blood, from the wound of the man she reflexively stabbed when he surprised her in a burglary, sprays across the screen. It almost seems to be actually stuck to the glass, and it sends a chill down Yanni's spine. She knows all too well what agony each day of a junkie's life can be.

As Yanni watches the end of her movie, the tension in Henry's New Jersey drama is gradually building.

Submerged in darkness, the aperture of Henry's anus is like a morning glory that shrivels and closes in the evening. Even Bob's powerful white fingers have difficulty probing inside to dig out, one by one, the tightly puckered folds.

Bob's necktie and trousers lie on the floor intertwined with Henry's jeans and sweaty T-shirt. A checkered handkerchief, its creases protruding at crazy angles, floats there on the carpet. A pocket watch sits upside-down, its dial facing the earth and its stainless steel back exposed to the universe. The faint *chock, chock* sound is not the cry of the dead moth or the rustling of trees, but the melody of time being measured and carved, a message the watch sends to the earth's core, rather than to the two men above.

A fountain pen reclines next to the watch, incapable of writing so much as the two men's initials. It's empty, the last of its ink having dried even as the summer sun was draining the last drops of juice from the blossoms of yellow lupine in the garden.

The ticket stub to a movie Henry saw the week before in Times Square lies crumpled up with a dollar bill. Three quarters and several dimes in the pocket of Bob's discarded trousers jingle together. This though no one has touched them.

Everything in the room begins to move in a halting, vertiginous swirl with a *chock, chock* like the sound of the watch, and the ceiling seems about to collapse under the weight of the sky. The walls too are contracting, and Henry imagines them falling inward out of the darkness.

Hundreds of clusters of crystal fruit and blossoms dangle uselessly about the unlit lamps of the chandelier. With each breath of breeze through the open window the little jewels quiver, evoking a faint fragrance of flowers. Their stone corollas clack together from time to time. Startling one another with the sound.

One of the crystal flowers begins to sway all by itself, and the carpet on the floor suddenly expands in every direction. The penis of a huge tree in the garden is sent flying as the carpet spreads out with breathtaking speed toward the four corners of the earth, overturning cities, mountains, rivers, swallowing up all the anger and discord in the world, and finally soaring beyond the horizon and weaving itself into the sky. Through half-open eyes Henry watches as the pattern on the carpet is dyed and embossed with the dust of stars.

In the garden outside, claret-colored asters, clematises, and golden nasturtiums panic as they're mowed down in this deranged phantasmal sketchbook. They fall by the thousands, heads severed, blood spurting out and soaking into the carpet. A hellish scene. A ruined landscape painting.

Henry looks on in a daze as the horse of madness gallops full tilt out of this landscape into his drug-starved body and dashes through his screaming veins like a phantom slasher.

A flock of deathbirds flies in a circle above his head. He watches as the formation contorts, as if the birds are trying to spell out something in the sky. The circle rearranges itself into something else, and now he sees it clearly: the symbol for death.

Beyond the birds, the great river has overflowed its banks; the flood rises to reach the roofs of the hustlers grotto, and the youths there, having never learned to swim, are drowning, thrashing and writhing about in agony before succumbing to merciless death. There's no one to retrieve and bury the bodies: those who stand at the end of civilization do not know enough to rue or recoil from death.

In the midst of his hallucination, Henry discovers a whirling, windblown panorama. He pursues this dazzling vision, his flesh panting with lunacy and shuddering with need for the drug that is its daily bread. His physiology tugs relentlessly at his senses, demanding the destruction of everything visible. There, on a bitter hilltop the light brown color of diacetyl morphine, poppies bloom as far as the eye can see. Henry makes a mad dash for those preternatural Turkish fields, straddling the horse that gallops through his veins and riding riotously through the flowers.

Now he lies supine among the poppies and gazes up at the sky. Even the clouds, transformed into dollar bills, have come looking for poppies to buy. A small white knob-headed creature, after crawling and poking brazenly about his crotch and buttocks, worms its way into the hole in his smooth dark-skinned crevice. His anus begins instantly to convulse as the yellow excreta in his bowels compact, increasing the pressure on his intestinal wall.

"I love you," Bob whispers into the black ear and gently takes the black face in his hands, his mouth once again seeking out the bright red strawberry lips that bloom there.

With Bob's penis inside him, Henry tries desperately to suppress the nausea that surges from stomach to throat. Maintaining its foothold in his anus the small white animal flits in and out, licking at his internal organs.

Henry groans. The little slug moves slowly up and down at first, but gradually gains strength and begins to run amok, ramming against the soft inner walls.

The night deepens.

Spasms of internal petals. Sheets sucking up the drops of sweat that exude from every gland. Two bodies aswim in the endless flow of perspiration. The waste in Henry's tightly packed rectum rushing to flee his body.

A rustle of leaves outside the window melts into

the tenderness of inner petals and sends up splashes of spray. Each individual hair around the damp hole adheres to the skin. The drip, drip of sticky liquid. The smell of this ooze chases after the purple cigarette smoke that has long since disappeared into the woods, climbing the treetops.

    The white penis shivers with ecstasy. Bob's slug shudders and squirms as his own wet warmth mixes with the yellow excreta issuing from the black hole beneath him, and a noisome odor fills their nostrils.

    The sad dying embers of lust summon up an illusory highway stretching from the silent woods outside to the ends of the universe, a highway wide enough for a speeding Porsche. Cars of every color and hue race over its surface. Headlights sniff out each hole in the trees of the forest. Strobelike flashes of illuminated space. Dryads are roused, one by one, from sleep. Outside the car window the trees speed past and recede into darkness. The aroused passions burn reborn in the cores of the trees and are left behind, forgotten now by the Porsche. Bob's semen continues to spurt toward the terminal station of oblivion. The dryads, their skin covered with feces, fly past the window, gleaming and sparkling golden in the night. White drops of semen snag on the uppermost twigs of a beech tree and drip, plopping, to cling to the branches below, then drip again to crawl down the bark, drawn toward the center of the earth.

    At blinding speed the road to the terminus overtakes all the visions imprinted on Henry's closed eyelids. The illusory highway twists and bucks, writhing over the surface of the earth. The car flips, its wheels pointed toward heaven and spinning uselessly. Henry strains his eyes to study the outcome of this drug-starved accident.

The hallucinated scenery. Trees, uprooted by the weight of the flipping car and the force of the collision, fall to the ground. The car itself is smashed to pieces. Branches split, then break. A beech raises its black arms to heaven and screams. Tire tracks are wrenched from the asphalt. A broken steering wheel. The driver's thirst burns his throat. The black well in the dark valley, long thought to be dry, fills with Bob's white jism. The mouth of the well overflows, eroding the ruined landscape with the force of a flood, turning everything white.

White covering the metallic silver glint of the steering wheel, white discoloring little by little, from left to right, the red plastic upholstery. The white bed sheets rising like smoke in the darkness. White erasing the pink polka-dot pattern of a blue parasol on the seat of the Porsche.

White erasing the scenery as far as the eye can see. When the car flips and rolls from the highway, black shadows tumble and crash, uprooted by its wheels. Beyond them, the great tree of the forest stretches its own long shadow over the face of the earth. As it falls, even the golden shit stuck to its bark turns white. Bob's white penis tree is ripped, root and branch, from the forest and out of Henry's vision.

Henry sees himself standing in the midst of this nightmarish scene and shivers. In his ill-omened hand he notices something that glitters a bright sports-car silver. The semen dogging him through the night continues to flow incessantly, entwining itself around the jackknife in his hand and dripping down on the carpet.

For one moment all the stars cease to shine. And

as they lose their light, Bob's raw, warm little animal separates from his body. The unattached clump of meat rolls over the highway, bumps against a rock, and comes to a stop.

Henry's butterfly soul, having flitted to the far shore of junk withdrawal and back, remembered itself with one final flutter and settled down to rest. But it was too late. Before returning to him, here in this world, his jackknife had already crossed the river of catastrophe.

It had all happened in the wink of an eye. Bob fell in a heap to the foot of the bed with both hands covering his groin. Emitting a low, gurgling moan.

All the fresh red blood that stained the edge of the knife began to change color as it was smothered with the whiteness of sperm. Henry, seeing the blood spurt from the fickle white manstem of love, sank into a sense of languorous pleasure, as if dipping into a sea of white powdered heroin, his fingers absently toying with the white blood.

The blood ate whitely away at the darkness around it, stained the torn petals of the flowers in the carpet, rocked the clumps of crystal in the chandelier, and continued to flow without surcease.

The white blood flowed over the two men's sexual discord, surged to the window, and assailed the billions of points of starlight that glittered in the sky above. Soon all the stars of heaven were frantically cloaking their glow in blood that gushed from the penis.

The two men had been floating and swimming in a sea of sperm and blood, but now Bob had run out of strength and drowned. Those eyes that had shone with lust and yearning would never blink again.

Henry, regaining his senses, rose up from the white sea of death.

Casually tossing the jackknife aside, he groped about on the floor for his jeans and put them on, then opened the door to the adjoining bathroom and switched on the light. He turned on the faucet next to the toilet and washed Bob's blood from his hands and arms. He wasn't the least bit concerned with where in the room Bob's member had fallen.

Perhaps he'd stepped on the severed organ as he hurried to put on his jeans. Perhaps it lay on the carpet somewhere. With the chandelier unlit, the adjoining room of death was obscure and indistinct, and as long as Henry touched nothing, perhaps nothing in there really existed.

Meanwhile, in Manhattan, Yanni had finished watching her movie and turned off the TV. She sat crosslegged on her bed with a razor and a book upon which she was cutting hashish into fine little pieces, mixing it with the tobacco of an unraveled cigarette, and using a little rolling machine to create a "nicktail." She lit it with a match and had taken one drag when the telephone beside the bed rang. She picked up the receiver and heard Henry's voice. Her clock said 12:30.

"Hey, darlin'," he said, speaking quickly, "my customer, his son just arrived at Kennedy Airport from Los Angeles and called the house here. So he has to go to the airport to meet him right away. So we be doin' it over again next week. The job's temporarily postponed, yeah. It's summer vacation, see, so he's gonna be in New York for a week or so, I guess. So Mr. Greenberg says he gotta show him around, you know.

So he gonna give me a ride back to Manhattan, uptown, now. He gotta go straight to the airport after that."

Was it only Yanni's imagination, or was Henry's voice rather shrill and nervous?

"Oh yes?" Yanni said, her Chinese accent showing. "Let me say hello to Mr. Greenberg. How it's going? You two hit it off?"

When she asked him again to put Bob on the phone, Henry hurriedly replied:

"Ah, he went down to the garage to get the car. He's not here. I'll see you at your apartment 'bout an hour."

And quickly hung up the phone.

Leaking through the spaces between the blinds, the red neon sign of Keefe's, a restaurant across the street, filled the room with stripes.

With the lights turned out, each piece of furniture was uniformly dyed with red stripes that vanished only to reappear at the whim of the sign's electricity.

There, amid the blinking neon, the voice of a rock singer pierced Yanni's temples.

> *Boy and boy, boy and boy*
> *Just met today*
> *No more to say*
> *Dance in the air, the sack and the pole*
> *Yeah, yeah, yeah, yeah*
> *Insert planet Penis and kiss*
> *Running too fast, moving too slow*
> *Just a street corner, just for today*
> *Meeting to make the bedsprings creak,*
>   *man on man*
> *Gimme a dollar, stick it in my pocket*

Night love glitters, hey, baby
C'mon, gay boy, Christopher
See you again tomorrow, after sunset
Yeah, yeah, yeah, yeah

The song on the radio played on. Reflecting that Henry would be showing up soon, Yanni took a bottle of milky liquid from the table next to her bed and rubbed the lotion on her amber skin. She caught a hint of sweet-smelling daphne buds in its fragrance, which blossomed into an image of the harbor of Hong Kong, the place of her birth. In her mind, the Orient was always a quiet place. At some point, as she listened to the radio, nodding, her dreams began to wander among the harbor lights of her Chinese hometown.

How much time had passed?

When Yanni opened her eyes to the urgent pounding on her door, the first thing she saw, backlit by the streetlight in the square window frame, was the bird's nest of Henry's hair, like a black thunder cloud.

Henry looked tired and out of sorts but went through the motions of paying respect, lightly kissing her small mouth. Then, with no further ado, he said, "Hey, darlin', lend me your needle."

He roughly yanked open the drawer of the desk next to her bed, pulled out her works, and rolled up his sleeve. Seeing she had little choice, Yanni handed him the heroin she kept hidden in a shoe beneath her bed. As he inserted the needle in his arm, he said:

"Mr. Greenberg and I decided to do our deal next week, seven days. I won't mess it up, I promise. So gimme a little advance, will ya? Listen ..."

Yanni could scarcely believe her ears. He said he wanted his entire cut—all four hundred dollars—right now. But if she didn't give it to him, strung out as he was, he was likely to go berserk.

As soon as he'd coerced her into giving him the money, Henry dashed out the door, without so much as a glance back at her. Yanni had always suspected that he gave her the loverboy treatment, complete with sex, only out of deference to her as his boss—in order to grease the wheels for money and work.

"Oriental girls are the best," he'd often tell her. "I'd much rather make it with a yellow woman than a white woman. Me, I like the petite, exotic type of lady. This homo shit is grotesque, man, makes me sick. Fuckin' faggots, God's gonna punish 'em all, make their assholes rot away. If He don't, I will. Go around the world stickin' red-hot pokers up all their asses."

Though with his next breath he might ask her to fix him up with a customer, once he got started bashing gays there was no end to it. Yet it wasn't as if he had a burning passion for Yanni, or women in general, either. Yanni, with her hip-length black hair, dark almond eyes, and feline grace, was precisely the type he claimed to be wild about, but the truth is that his heart was empty to the core. Nor were Yanni's feelings for Henry anything like love. Her own heart was so full of hatred for men, in fact, that renting out their bodies to others gave her tremendous satisfaction—in more than just a business sense.

As a little girl in Hong Kong, Yanni had lost her virginity to her own father, who'd raped her in the bath. From then on he'd forced himself upon her regularly. Eventually there'd been a pregnancy that she'd had to terminate in the third month at the hands of an unlicensed abortionist. By no means, therefore, was she unaware of the malice behind her efforts to match up young canaries with pederasts.

It was true she had some sympathy for Henry, however, if only because he was a "nigger" in a racist country. This though his black skin, normally a disadvantage, gave him a leg up in the queer world. White men viewed Negro youths as an extremely desirable prize. Henry's blackness and considerable beauty inspired in Yanni a mixture of love and hate, and her feelings about doing business with him were ambiguous, like those of an art dealer selling a fine work of art. Nonetheless, to get money in exchange for beautiful young men—black or white—was all a glorious game to her.

Henry's apartment was near the Hudson River, closer to the piers than Yanni's place. About five blocks to the west. On the evening of the fifth day since she'd last seen Henry, after eating dinner at the gay bar GEEZE, she stopped by to call on him.

"Henry, are you home? It's me," she said, turning the knob and cracking open the door. Looking in, she saw him lying on his bed, dead to the world. The flickering strobe light wasn't on today.

He didn't wake up when she called to him, so she let herself in, her eyes falling upon the triangular hole in the corner of the window next to the bed.

Henry's naked black skin rose and fell with his breathing, the lower half of his body covered with a filthy sheet. The round, well formed black mounds of his buttocks, with their faintly purple gemlike luster, captivated Yanni's gaze. Today, too, through the broken window, the sun was setting over the New Jersey skyline. For some reason she'd forgotten to look up at the flaking grape-colored lion sculpture today as she ran up the steps.

She'd been somewhat concerned the past few days. Concerned, predictably enough, about Mr. Greenberg. As a small business courtesy, she'd called his summer house and his apartment in Manhattan to confirm the postponement of the seven-day deal, but no one had answered at either place. In all, she'd called four times and hadn't been able to reach him. That was odd. What could be going on? She could only imagine that he was busy playing the good father, entertaining the son from California he hadn't seen for so long.

But later, when she called his real estate firm on 42nd Street just to make sure, his secretary, a man named Michael, said that he hadn't showed up at the office for several days.

"I understand his son is in from California," Yanni said. "I suppose he's been busy showing him around?"

The secretary seemed surprised to hear this, however.

"Oh, is that right?" he said. "The truth is, I was a bit worried because he hasn't called in."

This conversation had bothered Yanni enough that she'd decided to visit Henry's apartment. She hiked up the skirt of her Chinese dress and sat crosslegged on the floor, biding her time for twenty or thirty minutes, only half expecting him to awaken. But as she sat looking up at the madder-red clouds in the sky beyond the broken triangle of glass, she slid gradually into the grip of a nameless dread.

Her eyes fell upon Henry's discarded jeans lying on the floor. Distractedly she pulled them closer and was fidgeting with the material when she felt something hard and solid inside the rear pocket. Wondering what it might be, she reached in with her fingers and brought out pieces of men's jewelry.

A platinum tiepin mounted with an opal surrounded by six diamonds. It was the outrageously flashy sort of item that gays favored and most straight men would never wear. Anyone could see at a glance that it belonged to a homosexual. And, she immediately thought, not just any homosexual, but a wealthy "buyer" type. Another object slipped from her fingers and fell to the floor with a clatter. A ring. She silently scooped it up and shot a glance at Henry. On the bed above her, his chest rising and falling with the breath of sleep, he was still oblivious to her presence. Yanni breathed a small sigh of relief.

The ring in her hand was plainly a man's as well. It was thick 18-karat gold, with a jadeite heart sparkling between two roses that identified the owner as gay. After she'd gazed at it for a moment, Yanni felt the blood drain from her face.

A scene from the recent past was replaying in her mind. She'd seen this ring before, during dinner at the Italian restaurant where she'd introduced Henry to Mr. Greenberg. Greenberg had been wearing it on his left ring finger. When he'd placed his elbows on the table and spoken to her, she'd briefly noted what a lovely color the jadeite was. It was the same ring. There was no doubt about it. Yanni's heart froze.

There was a bulge in the other rear pocket of the jeans.

She reached in and pulled out several strips of paper.

Among them were two pawn tickets for the Bricker Brothers Pawn Shop. Smoothing out the wrinkles on one of them, she found it to be dated August 23. The twenty-third would be the day after Henry had come to her apartment so late at night, saying Greenberg had dropped him off.

Listed on the ticket was an 18-karat gold Swiss watch, and next to it was written "$900." A second pawn ticket listed a diamond ring for seven hundred. That made a total of sixteen hundred dollars. Smoothing out the wrinkles again and again, Yanni tried to think what to do. But her mind was in too much of a whirl. All that seemed clear was that Henry had stolen these things either from Mr. Greenberg's person or from a room in his summer house. The more she thought about it, the more certain she became. And judging from the fact that Greenberg had been missing for several days, it was probable that something had happened to him in conjunction with the theft.

If everything was as she imagined, she would have to get Henry to abscond to the Northwest, or Texas—or *someplace*—as soon as possible. It would be dangerous not to flee New York. If he remained here, there was no telling when the police might burst in.

Yanni stood up, closed the door to the room, and made sure it was locked.

She also shut the curtain over the window with the triangular hole.

To call the summer house in New Jersey from here would only be inviting trouble. It would be bad news if the police or Greenberg's secretary answered. Fortunately, when she'd called his office a few days earlier, she hadn't told the secretary her name. She and Greenberg had always conducted their business on his private phone.

Yanni had a splitting headache; her temples were throbbing, and her throat was suddenly so dry that she had no voice.

All the sweat glands in her body clamored for water. Hot and cold flashes ran down her back, as if she'd caught a chill. The tips of her hands and feet were moist with a cold sweat, and she felt she could no longer just sit there.

She took the key and went out of the room. Locking the door from the outside, she passed beneath the sculpture of the young lion, skittered down the steps, and ran to the delicatessen on the corner.

She purchased three small cartons of orange juice and some ice cream. Then, with her change, she bought the *New York Post* at a newsstand. The evening edition.

A breeze was finally blowing across the sky, cooling things down, and residents of the apartment buildings were sitting out on their stoops, watching the people go by.

The crimson lake hue that dyed the clouds was losing its brightness by the moment, turning them purple. Rain clouds appeared in one corner of the sky. A Dutch ship departed, sounding its whistle. The sound reverberated through the sky over this foreign land. Crew members came out on deck and waved toward the piers of Manhattan. On the piers, the boys the sailors had bought waved back. The ship slowly receded into the distance. Little by little, heavy gray clouds began to dominate the sky.

Yanni unlocked the door to Henry's room, and this time locked and bolted it from the inside. As she drank her juice she opened the newspaper and turned on the lamp. She leafed through the pages until she came to the city section, at which instant her blood seemed to flow backwards in her veins, as if she'd been electrocuted. A photo at the top of the page leaped out at her. A head shot of Mr. Greenberg. Beneath it was a photo of a large summer house surrounded by trees. Her breath caught in her throat.

"Robert Greenberg, President of Mayflower Realtors, Found Murdered," read the subhead beneath a banner headline that said, astonishingly:

SEVERED PENIS SUMMER HOUSE MYSTERY

Yanni grew so dizzy that the furniture before her and the carton of juice in her hand seemed to spin about the room. Her hands were trembling, and it was all she could do to steady herself by grabbing the iron leg of Henry's bed.

The headlines were all she could see. She hadn't the strength even to read the article. She looked up at Henry, still with his back to her, submerged in sleep. Mindlessly she guzzled the orange juice, but no matter how much she drank, her insides remained as parched as a desert.

There was no doubt about it now. Her worst fears had been realized.

She would have to help him escape. Tonight.

She pulled herself together, spread the paper out on the floor, and pored over the words.

The things in the article that had the biggest impact on her were as follows:

The victim, Mr. Greenberg, had been found completely nude. His penis had been severed at the base, and the severed penis was found on the floor beside the bed. A jackknife covered with blood that lay discarded on the bed was considered a major piece of evidence, and authorities were hurrying to conduct tests, hoping that fingerprints on it would lead to a quick arrest. It was also learned that late on the night of the crime a Mr. Jenkins, who owned a summer house in the vicinity of Greenberg's, had been approached by a young black man near the so-called Saint Neurosis intersection. Mr. Jenkins said he'd been driving with his wife when he was stopped by a handsome black hitchhiker of twenty-five or -six, whom he later dropped off at 59th Street and 8th Avenue.

Which meant that Henry had got a lift as far as 59th Street from this Mr. Jenkins, then perhaps caught another ride downtown.

Yanni began shaking Henry's shoulder violently.

He didn't respond. He was deep in a bottomless sleep.

Pushing and poking him had no effect, so Yanni pried open his eyelids with the fingers of her left hand. His pupils were as small as pinholes. This is not good, she thought.

His body was in some sort of abnormal state.

When she jerks awake and lifts her head, a pale light is showing through the slit between the curtains. She must have nodded off, overwhelmed as she was with fatigue and too many emotions. She shakes Henry again. This time he wearily raises himself up, black buttocks first, and squints at his boss through a fog of dreams. Yanni smoothes the embroidered dragon on the front of her red Chinese dress as she rises to her feet. Flipping back her long and thick black hair, she silently holds the previous evening's *New York Post* out in front of him.

When his gaze falls on the page, Henry says nothing. His face shows not the slightest change of expression. Nor does Yanni, observing this, feel an urge to ask him anything. The two of them just sit there on the bed in a grim silence.

Not even they have any idea what they're thinking. The *Post* article and Greenberg's death aren't even on their minds at this point. They simply feel an overwhelming desire to get outside and breathe the fresh morning air.

They walk slowly along the street in the pale first light of dawn. A faint milk-colored curtain enfolds their little isle of stone. The city, empty even of dairy trucks, floats in the space between night and morning. The mists of dawn cling to the buildings on the skyline and restrain the air from moving. The moon, longing for the west, finally forsakes the island and falls to earth. Above the black tree-lined hill across the Hudson, mist devours the last of the moon's transparent light and spreads milkwhite paint over the shrinking surface of the planet, muffling the sounds of the city.

Parting this creamlike gauze a young boy approaches, his wheatstraw-colored hair rippling as he gives a wholesome toss of his head. His eyes are eyes that have seen no more than a decade of life. Innocent deep pure eyes. He peers into Yanni's and Henry's faces, then speaks.

"What's beyond the milky curtain?"

The outline of the boy's body is without shading, like a figure in a crayon landscape, a thin two-dimensional form. Startled, they look more closely, only to see the wheatstraw hair of this shadowless boy disappear in the mist. All that remains is the sound of his breath whispering something in their ears. A slight but pungent scent of green wheat fields wafts in the air.

A silver wiremesh trashcan sits on the now-deserted corner, idly nursing its load of refuse. A scraggly cat leaps up to its rim and vanishes into the filthy interior. A rustling sound sucks up a fragment of air, attempting to clothe itself in morning. But the morning sun declines to show and sits holding its breath, far off behind the many veils of turbid air, refusing to move. The earth has stopped.

Astonished, the two of them press their hands to the ground and confirm their suspicion: the earth has ceased to turn. Parting with their hands the sweetsour semen-colored curtain that enshrouds the island, they press onward until they find their progress blocked by no less an obstacle than the Empire State Building. The shock of this seeps through the cracks in their hearts, and they look up to see the tip of the great tower hidden in riotous black clouds that roil and surge while the wind, howling, assaults the thousand windows.

That gem-studded nightless castle, the skyscraper Henry remembers seeing from a window in the New Jersey forest, has completely lost its sparkle. It's now a skeletal structure the color of old straw that gleams in patches between the gray clouds and sways expansively in space. The mist crawls over the ground, resisting the upward pull.

The sight takes their breath away. The day that never dawned. The stairway leading to the top of the tower is, oddly enough, not concrete. A small white door opens and calls to them. Its rough wood grain is split and splintered. It looks as if it has weathered the wind and rain on this stone-carved island for thousands of years. They stand at the threshold and instinctively look up at the roiling sky.

With their field of vision circumscribed by dark clouds, their conception of the moon, the sun, the stars, is sealed as well, and try as they might they cannot bring those shapes to mind. What were they like, those wonderful lights? The faces, smells, and tastes of the celestial bodies, and the universe itself, are no longer accessible to their senses. The eyes of this man and woman, even with the blindman's cane of the soul, have lost the ability to perceive those eternally shining lights anywhere in the future. Perhaps all there has ever been is the fragrance of youth.

Henry takes Yanni's hand and they begin to climb step by step toward the boundless sky. The stairs to the top of the tower are numberless, stacked higher than the mind can comprehend. The ascent seems endless. Now that the earth has stopped, the sun will never shine upon this tower again.

The passageway to the top. Crushed fragments of blood-splattered fruit stick red to the window at each floor, where crows peck at them furiously. The birds, famished, smash the bright red bits of fruit with all the strength at their disposal, opening thousands upon thousands of holes in the window panes.

Rats with distended bellies flee before them, startled by the sound of their footsteps. Abdomens swollen not by pregnancy but by the proliferation of cancer cells scrape over the floor as they walk. One rat falls behind; it has lost half its hind leg to a tumor that drips pus where it has eaten through. A sticky film the color of cloudy egg yolk covers each step and sticks to the soles of their bare feet.

The floating transient dream of life on Manhattan Island, that unsinkable ship of worldly pleasures that once wove fabulous patterns of passion and love in the light of red lanterns encrusted with diamonds and rubies—this dream has been cruelly transformed into towering ruins that bring only grief to the hearts of the man and woman now climbing these stairs to the sky.

Yanni's face presses against something soft and sticky. She draws back and looks at Henry. The dark skin of his face, too, is embossed with a virginal white spider's web, a net of countless octagonal meshes. Its work destroyed by the human being it has trapped, a long-legged spider continues silently to spin its beautiful silky white thread over Henry's face.

Near the top of the tower they look down toward the earth to see the semenlike morning mist floating far below, reaching only as high as the twentieth floor and showing no sign of lifting. Turning their gaze upward, they watch the clouds gathering again, summoned by a brewing storm. Perhaps to bring rain to cleanse the corrupt and desecrated surface of the earth.

Finally, out of breath and all but crawling on hands and knees, they reach the top.

With their feet on the last step they see before them another worn and coarse-grained splintered door, open to the desolate sky. They entered the first door to leave the earth; this is the exit to heaven. The doorway is for all the world like a sacred Oriental shrine, and for one hallucinatory moment Yanni imagines herself back in her birthplace, Hong Kong.

They step out onto the balcony that spreads beyond the door. Able at last to fill their lungs with air. But nothing has changed: morning never arrived. The still earth maintains its grim silence and gives no indication of moving. How can morning come when the earth no longer turns on its axis?

Looking down from the balcony they see seagulls flying in and out of the sooty mist. Their white feathers, covered with the dirt and dust of civilization, are tattered and gray, pathetic.

The floor of the balcony, reflecting the dark clouds above, shines dully, like tarnished silver. The rays of light pierce Yanni's eyes and again she looks away, toward the copper tiles on the roof of St. Patrick's Cathedral flashing and blinking eerily between the clouds. The tiles glow and change color in the wind. Far off, dimly visible through the clouds, is the ridgeline of buildings on Wall Street.

The seagulls flock together over the matchbox-shaped UN Building and fly off toward an island in the East River. They've apparently gone to scavenge crumbs of bread from the gardens of the crowded geriatric hospital there and the decaying old-folks' home next door.

When the cloudy sky shifts suddenly and the floor of the balcony ceases to shine, it's transformed into a vast, unbroken sea of rubbish. Empty Coca-Cola bottles, hamburger scraps, and lumps of discarded chewing gum rise up in relief. Fruits of material civilization, left behind by the daily sightseers.

Yanni cuts her toe on an empty can, and blood spurts out.

Rats have climbed up here as well. Dragging their abnormal swollen bellies, they slither about scrounging for food.

Seeing a rat at her feet, Yanni experiences something midway between nausea and vertigo. Juice and undigested food heave up from her stomach and spill out on top of the rat. The front of her red Chinese dress is splattered with vomit. The embroidered dragon, flicking its tongue, greedily licks it clean.

Henry gazes at the clouds in the distance with empty eyes. Sweat pours from his neck down his chest and T-shirt. The view, the clouds, the rain-heavy layers of sky are all disconnected from his pupils and brain; all one vast indistinct unknowable object retreating into the distance. Nothing has any relation to him whatsoever; a thin translucent curtain cuts him off from the external world.

He repeatedly wipes the sweat from his neck. His breath comes in rough hurried gasps.

Not even a trace of the black shadowy New Jersey forest enters his field of vision; there are only the immobile clouds gathered before him. All phenomena retreat farther and farther from view. His own body is not a thing that really exists: the only traces left of it are the cold drops of sweat that pour from his hands and feet and the beating of his heart, and he loses himself in the sense of his soul separating and drifting in space.

His body and mind are two distinct entities, as if he's been thrown into a vacuum: a prisoner surrounded by the curtain of depersonalization.

No sentiment, no emotions, no connection to anything. The scenery. The external world.

As his body languishes imprisoned behind this curtain, he feels his spirit dance up and out of his body.

Yanni, after following the seagulls with her gaze, glances back at the floor to find that the clouds are reflected there again, erasing the sea of trash in a silver glow. Casting her eyes over the silvery void, she finally manages to suppress her nausea.

But the black figure of Henry is no longer there where it's supposed to be, in the corner of the void. The space he was standing in is empty.

She gasps. Surely, she tells herself, the clouds' reflection has merely screened him from view. Once the clouds move again, the outline of his body will reappear, along with the Coke bottles and scraps of paper.

Yanni turns her eyes once more to the shifting clouds. As they move, the silvery reflection fades from the balcony floor, restoring the various shapes there. But the mass that was Henry's body is nowhere to be seen.

It crosses her mind that she's merely imagining this; her eyes are tired and her vision hazy. She tries to refocus her eyes by peering at the wood grain of the door to the stairwell they ascended from earth just moments before. Then, bracing herself, she looks back to where Henry ought to be standing. Her heart stops. His body has vanished from that space. Yanni runs to the railing and looks down.

In the milk-colored mist a single black spot. Falling.

The spot grows smaller and smaller, until it's just a dark speck dissolving into the mist.

The crows that were pecking away at their blood-red fruit lift up into the air as one, and with their backs to heaven they form a ring and chase the black speck toward earth.

foxgloves

of

central park

The tips of the foxgloves telescope endlessly. Any number of stalks intertwine in a netlike mesh and writhe like snakes. The tips blur and vanish beyond the horizon. Pluck one of the flowers and its purplish-yellow juice fills your hand to overflowing and drips to the absorbent earth.

This vision terrified Shimako. She touched her forehead and found it coated with a cold sweat. Looking around, she saw the trees of Central Park shaking as if in an 8.0 earthquake. *Was* it an earthquake? But people were strolling calmly about.

Which meant it must be one of her episodes.

When she looked up at the sky, dogs were running through the air. The exaggerated shaking of the trees made her feel as if her feet were about to slip out from under her. Yes, the episodes are starting again, Shimako thought, taking from her handbag two of the white pills the doctor had prescribed and heading for a nearby drinking fountain. The earth shook as she walked, and she felt a bottomless anxiety. Just her luck to have an episode in the middle of Central Park.

Glancing at the bed of foxgloves, she could see

that the tips of the flowers had continued to elongate and now drooped to lie along the horizon. The clusters of blossoms multiplied endlessly.

In the midst of the foxglove hallucination, she saw two people fighting:

Herself and her mother, Sakuko. Sakuko hit her daughter as hard as she could.

"I never should've had you!" she shouted. "One mistake in contraception and I end up with a child. That child was you. You're someone who never should have been born!"

She tore Shimako's hair and scratched her face.

Such was the primal image of her mother that had been repeatedly impressed on Shimako over the course of many years. This vexing memory was all her mother was to her now, and it came back to her even in the midst of hallucinations. Her mother's husband, Shuzo, had kept a mistress and was rarely at home. Nor was he content with just having a mistress but continued to go after every woman he saw, and this played havoc with Sakuko's nerves. Shimako bore the brunt of her mother's hysterical reactions.

Watching her parents fight since infancy had left its mark on Shimako; her heart was a whirlpool of pain and insecurity.

She'd been to psychiatrists even before coming to New York. During a period when she'd seen her parents fight every day, she'd developed such a dizzying fear of knives, for example, that she couldn't bear even to look at one.

There was never so much as a single day of peace.

Perhaps it was because of the strife-filled atmosphere of the household that Shimako's eldest brother, Yoshikichi, had become an alcoholic, wandering the streets all night drinking and earning a reputation as the town ne'er-do-well. The stifling environment at home had instilled in him a seething rage that he took out on his little sister.

Yoshikichi was a devoted torturer of animals: he threw stones at every cat he saw, and those he could catch he strung up by the hind legs. He was also quite thorough in his torment of Shimako. He'd refuse to permit her to eat, for example, on the grounds that she'd spent the entire day loafing about, reading books; if she dared to wear a yellow sweater, he'd run around shouting that the family was raising a shameless little whore.

Shimako had begun having hallucinations at fifteen or sixteen. She'd go to the violet-covered meadow behind the house and spend hours on end chatting with the violets.

She could talk with animals as well. It was always the animals who initiated the conversations.

The violets looked like human faces, and spoke to her individually. In human voices.

One day a dog approached Shimako. When she and the dog spoke together, she became terrified by the realization that her voice had become a dog's voice. She ran back home, shut herself in the closet, and sat there trembling.

Things she was looking at would slowly recede away from her, into the distance. The doctor called it "depersonalization disorder."

Shimako's psychiatrist said her home environment was just too unhealthy. He recommended a change of surroundings as soon as possible. Otherwise, he said, she would only get worse.

Shimako ran away from home with only enough money for a one-way train ticket to Tokyo. She headed straight for the boardinghouse of a friend from the girls' school she'd attended. After settling in there, she began going to a psychiatrist in the city. If not for her friend's financial help, Shimako would probably have starved to death.

Once she'd learned that a friend of her friend had a connection to the United States, Shimako began thinking she'd like to go overseas. Her friend's friend lived in New York, and Shimako first came to America as a live-in helper in that woman's house.

Coming to New York didn't cure her illness, but it did help her realize her greatest wish: to get as far as possible from that detestable family of hers.

Having come to this country as a housekeeper, no sooner had Shimako arrived in New York than she was put to work baby-sitting the children, helping with shopping, preparing dinners, and washing dishes.

She'd left for the U.S. without saying a word to her own family. She hoped never to see them again as long as she lived.

Thinking of the countless insults she'd suffered from them—particularly her mother, who'd brought her into the world only to tell her to her face, again and again, that she wished she'd never been born—now filled Shimako with indignation.

Growing up, she'd always liked to read, both books and newspapers. If caught reading, however, she was likely to receive a quite literal and painful kick in the pants. The books would be torn to shreds. Ripped apart and thrown away.

Her elder brothers were just as violent as her mother. There were two of them. She'd never seen much of her father. Whenever he was home, he was certain to get into a scuffle with her mother. The main source of conflict was the fact that, while her father would dress to the nines and sprinkle himself with perfume before going to visit his mistress, her mother was left to manage both the housework and the general store they owned, too busy even to concern herself with her appearance. Her father would help himself to the coffers his wife's labor had filled and use the money to support his mistress. Though her mother wore the same kimono every day of the year, her father strutted about in the most fashionable and modern attire of the times—walking stick, derby hat, and checkered suit. He was such a dandy that people he passed on the street would actually turn to look back at him. And where did he find perfume, living so far out in the country?

Shimako hated her parents' fights, and everything else they did. And she hated her eldest brother's teasing and bullying even more. She'd come to New York intending never to see any of them again.

In New York, as in Tokyo, she didn't write so much as a single letter home. She hadn't communicated with her family at all for two years now.

But even after coming to New York, she continued to hallucinate. Her psychiatrist here said she suffered from anxiety and obsessive-compulsive neuroses as a result of the emotionally unstable environment in which she'd spent her early childhood. She went to see him once a week to receive medication.

The family she lived with were middle class and owned a midtown Japanese restaurant called Arita.

They had three small children, and taking care of them was Shimako's main job. The parents had been especially eager to find someone from Japan to care for the children.

Shimako had come to Central Park today because it was the one day of the week she had off.

She was by herself. It would remain a mystery to her how she managed to return to the Arita's house. She was in a trance-like state.

The road in Central Park rose up before her, like a path ascending a forest knoll, and Shimako involuntarily let out a cry. Looking into the distance from atop the knoll she could see the horizon far, far away. She sank to her haunches, unable to move.

The sun had already gone down over New Jersey, and dusk was rapidly gathering.

Shimako's doctor had often pointed out how noisy and stressful the city was. He recommended she go somewhere quiet, like a farming community, to recuperate.

Caring for the children was hard work. The youngest child still messed his diapers, and cleaning up after him was particularly trying.

The doctor was always kind to Shimako and, knowing of her unfortunate background and lack of money, didn't charge her for consultations.

She'd made it to New York, but the future was still dark as night. What's more, her nervous condition wasn't improving.

The doctor knew of some people who ran a farm in New Jersey specializing in Japanese-style vegetables, and he said they were looking for help. A quiet, natural environment like that would be good for Shimako's illness, he once again advised her.

It was true that she was nearly going mad in the Arita's house with three children clinging to her skirts.

So Shimako moved to New Jersey.

The farm in New Jersey was quite a large one. They grew daikon radishes, eggplants—not American-style eggplants, but the smaller Japanese variety—scallions and adzuki beans, and sold them to the Japanese community in New York.

One day, as Shimako pulled a young daikon from the earth, the radish's long root entwined itself around the palm of her hand. It covered her hand completely. Startled, she tried to pry it off, only to find that it stuck to her other hand as well. Try as she might, she could not get it off her hands. In fact, her entire field of vision began to fill with daikon images. Shimako crumpled to the ground and lay face down. She was petrified with fear.

Infinitely repeated images of a given object would fill her field of vision. This visual effect grew stronger each day. She'd see a basket full of freshly picked eggplants, and suddenly she'd be boxed in, with mountains of eggplants on every side.

Now a voice began to call to her: *Shimako ... Shimako!* Even as she looked about and saw no one there, the voice continued to call her name. Her ears felt as if they would burst.

Shimako let out a scream and ran into the house of the farmer, Mr. Hijikata.

"Someone is after me!" she cried.

Seeing Shimako in such a frenzied state, with her hair in disarray, Mrs. Hijikata spoke to her firmly, though in the gentlest possible tones.

"You've lost your mind," she said. "I've been watching you. I thought there was something wrong. You see things, don't you, Shimako? And you hear voices. You should be in a hospital getting treatment. You must talk to your doctor, the one who introduced you to us—Dr. Takeyama."

That evening Dr. Takeyama came with his wife to get Shimako.

Though less than pleased with the prospect, Shimako had to be admitted to the public psychiatric ward at Bellevue.

She was unable to forget the daily kindnesses shown her by the Hijikatas in New Jersey and thought constantly about returning there.

This time her condition was diagnosed as schizophrenia. An acquaintance from her first days in New York, Martha, came to visit with her boyfriend and brought flowers. She was a pharmacist at Stuyvesant Hospital and one of Shimako's very few friends.

"You must be patient," she told Shimako. "Relax. Take your time recuperating."

It was one thing to tell Shimako to relax, but the psychiatric ward at Bellevue was even more hellish than the hospital in the film *The Snake Pit*. It was utter bedlam.

There was every imaginable sort of patient, from black prostitutes who'd gone mad doing too many drugs to manic depressives, who in their manic phases were perhaps the most boisterous and out of control.

It was all but impossible to sleep at night. Dozens of patients were crammed into one room, each behaving as he or she pleased, which made for a truly nightmarish atmosphere.

Dr. Takeyama felt sorry for Shimako.

"I didn't want to put you in a place like this, but it's the only hospital that's free of charge. Mental institutions are all expensive in America."

Little by little Shimako resigned herself to being in this infernal place. The building, whose red-brick exterior made it look restful and sedate, was anything but restful inside. It might have been hell itself.

The overwhelming majority of patients were drug addicts. Addicts in the last stages of their disease. They never sat still, and were given to random screaming. The walls seemed on the verge of collapsing from the sheer noise and incredible energy they generated. Shimako passed each day here in a bewildered sort of daze.

She was also tormented by her depersonalization, the most pronounced symptom of which was a sense of tremendous physical distance between herself and those around her.

It was as if a curtain separated her from the outer world and she had no direct connection to anything; there were even times when she was completely incapable of understanding the voices of people speaking to her. She complained of this to Dr. Takeyama, who visited her occasionally.

But what bothered her more were the voices that

came from out of nowhere and ordered her about. They dictated her every move. Do this, do that, you mustn't do so-and-so ...

Once, a voice told her:

"Hit the girl next to you."

She did as she was told, and it caused a great deal of trouble. She and the girl got into a terrible fight. The voice was sometimes that of Sakuko, sometimes that of Shuzo, and sometimes that of her brother Yoshikichi.

At times the voices criticizing and abusing her were so overwhelming that she felt as if she were going to lose her mind completely, and she'd begin to scream:

"Ahh! Ah! Ahh!"

Shimako couldn't take any more. She could no longer bear the tremendous burden in her heart.

Seeing no one but crazy people all day was enough to make her lose her bearings entirely. But she hadn't the money to move to a better hospital. She hadn't so much as a dollar to her name.

She'd reached the most extreme state of poverty. Life in the hospital was such bedlam, however, that there was scarcely a moment to think about how to improve her situation.

Patients of every description wandered back and forth, or sat slumped over, heads bowed, for whole days at a time. Others shouted all day long at the top of their lungs. Shimako didn't imagine that her illness had particularly improved since she'd been here.

It even seemed as if the voices she heard so constantly had got worse than ever.

The voices roared so loudly that it hurt. But not even covering her ears with her hands did any good.

The voices not only continued but seemed to be coming from inside her skull.

"Die, you!" they sometimes said. Or:

"I'm going to beat you to death!" or "Don't move from that spot all day!" or "Kill him!" or "Hit that nurse!" Sometimes it was a man's voice, sometimes a woman's, inciting her to do all sorts of things.

She was also menaced by visual hallucinations.

In the big room of the women's ward a field of Shasta daisies appeared, waving in the wind, their white corollas multiplying endlessly. Not just on the walls but spilling over to the floor and ceiling as well, until Shimako found herself buried among them and let out a scream.

A nurse came running.

"What happened?" she said, shaking Shimako by the shoulders.

With this, Shimako regained her senses, but all she could say to the nurse was:

"They're going to kill me!"

The nurse brought a doctor, and the two of them injected Shimako with a big, thick needle. Shimako then slept for four hours.

That evening Dr. Takeyama came by to check on her. Dr. Takeyama was on the board of the Japan Society of New York, which obliged him to look after Japanese students and other Japanese residents in the area.

"How are you doing?" he asked.

Shimako told him how the Shasta daisies had spread and how they had nearly destroyed her.

"I was scared, Doctor," she said, and he said he could well imagine she had been.

"Shimako," he said, "this is the worst mental

institution in the world. It's full of terminal drug addicts. To leave you in here much longer would only worsen your condition. I asked a friend of mine who runs a private hospital if he could help us out. He said he could probably accommodate one extra patient. What do you think? It's up to you, but I'd say this is an extraordinary opportunity. The mere fact that such a benevolent doctor exists in hardhearted old New York is practically a miracle in itself."

"Dr. Takeyama," she said, "take me there, please. The sooner I get out of this hellhole the better. I've been bearing up as well as I can, but I think this place only makes me even more emotionally disturbed."

So Shimako was moved to a double room in a private hospital in Queens. She was delighted just to have a little peace and quiet again.

The bedlam that had tormented her so in the old place now seemed little more than a bad dream.

Shimako loved the quiet new hospital.

She couldn't help feeling a bit guilty, however, about accepting such treatment when she couldn't pay so much as a single dollar.

"Doctor, are you sure it's all right for me to stay here when I don't have even a dollar to my name?"

"The head of this hospital has been kind enough to give us a special rate for you," Dr. Takeyama said, "and one of the directors of the Japan Society, a wealthy American lady, has agreed to cover the expense. So don't you worry about that for now. Just concentrate on getting well."

Shimako shared a room with a black woman of twenty-one or -two.

The woman spent each day talking to an imaginary person. Apparently someone spoke to her from some undefined place. She would answer or perhaps speak along with them, but it looked as if she were talking to herself. She didn't seem to pose any danger to others, however.

Out the window the skyline of Manhattan stood in bold relief against the blue sky. It looked like a fortress of concrete and stone.

It was discouraging to Shimako that though she'd come to New York to work she'd ended up living in psychiatric hospitals.

As for consultations, since Shimako had not been in the U.S. very long and her English was still quite shaky, she generally had to wait for Dr. Takeyama to show up and speak with her in Japanese.

A nurse came to check on her from time to time.

Thus far she hadn't spoken with the black woman who was her roommate. As before, the woman was submerged in her own world, incessantly conversing with someone who wasn't there.

Shimako, for her part, still suffered auditory and visual hallucinations. The one yelling at her now was her mother, Sakuko.

"If I hadn't given birth to the children of that cheating husband of mine I would have divorced him in nothing flat. Even when I was pregnant, with my belly bulging, he kept going to see his mistress. Taking our precious household money and not doing a lick of work, out gallivanting with women every day, from the third day of our marriage. Kill Daddy, Shimako. Don't think of him as your father."

To which her father replied:

"I'm willing to divorce at any time. Say the word and I'll leave tomorrow."

Shimako heaved a sigh. She'd run off as far as America to get away from the fighting, but the voices had followed her here, and she heard them now more than ever.

Every once in a while she would let out a scream. Each time she did, a nurse would come and restrain her, speaking to her in English. She would also bring medication, with water. What sort of medicine might it be?

From the grounds, you could see that the building was on a small rise, with a gentle slope fanning out around it, punctuated by flower beds full of blossoms. The summer sun shone down hard on the flowers, and some of them were wilted. A gardener came around to water them from time to time.

Shimako had grown deeply pessimistic about her future, thinking how difficult it would be now to go out and find work; looking ahead, all she could see were the flowers bursting into flame in the hot summer sun.

The tips of the flowers flickered, and smoke rose from the flames. Red and pink petals of mums were becoming charred and twisted. The fires were ascending the slope from the bottom, where they'd first flared up.

Shimako began shouting frantically:

"Fire! The garden's on fire!"

A nurse dressed all in white came running.

"There's no fire anywhere," she said, leading Shimako to her room. "You're seeing things. Let's go back to your room and get some sleep. OK?"

But Shimako continued to scream.

"The flower beds are burning! They really are! Our house will catch fire too! We've got to put it out, fast!"

"There's no fire," said the nurse. "Come, now. Let's take our medicine and have a little nap."

Her symptoms weren't showing much improvement. Shimako was still tormented by hallucinations and frequently lost all sense of identity.

Dr. Takeyama was talking with the director of the hospital, Dr. Kearn.

"She has a tendency for schizophrenic episodes," he said, "but it won't do for her to go back to Japan because her family situation is so bad. She was running away from home when she came here in the first place."

Dr. Kearn sympathized with Shimako.

"Most people who become ill," he said, "are products of troubled families."

Shimako wanted to die. She'd come to New York in high spirits, intending to work, but the illness she'd suffered in Japan had continued. What was she going to do?

When she consulted Dr. Takeyama about this, he tried to encourage her, saying:

"If you go back to Japan you'll have to have some sort of dealings with your family. We'll look after you here, so why not stay in America until you're well?"

Shimako had nowhere to go and little choice but to do as the doctor suggested. Her situation was such that there was simply no other place she could be.

It was as if she had no family at all.

But the delusions she suffered daily left her little time to be preoccupied with such thoughts.

For an entire day, everything she saw would look warped, misshapen; faces would appear on the surface of doors; an old man with a cane would come tottering out of the wall.

Looking out the window as dusk approached, she could see that all the flowers in the garden beds were wilted, drooping to the ground. For the life of her she couldn't understand why the flowers would have collapsed like that. When she called the nurse and asked about it, the nurse said:

"That's how you see them, but in fact there's nothing wrong with the flowers."

Shimako couldn't comprehend what was going on. Every day was filled with enigmas.

She had a strong desire to return to New Jersey and work on the Hijikata's farm, to earn her own way, but her illness would hardly allow such a course of action. It was all she could do to face each day in the hospital.

Dr. Takeyama seemed to think she'd need three or four years of treatment. But if this illness of hers could be cured in three or four years it would be a miracle. Shimako had a girl cousin who was also schizophrenic. The hospital she was in was like a hospital at the end of the world. The food was awful, and the facilities were the worst.

Yet the cousin had put up with those conditions for well over ten years. She was kept in a large room with all sorts of other patients, who cried and wailed incessantly. It was much like the psychiatric ward at Bellevue.

There were countless unfortunate people in this world. All of them persevered. Each had to endure the destiny that was his lot.

And there were any number of children who, like Shimako, had never known the atmosphere of a normal home and family.

Shimako felt boundless gratitude to all those who'd helped her gain admission to this hospital. If it weren't for them, she'd probably be getting even worse, in that snake pit at Bellevue.

The director, Dr. Kearn, came to see her from time to time and ask how she was feeling.

Her black roommate had finally begun to open up to Shimako, and they occasionally spoke together now. She said she'd been there half a year. She was schizophrenic. Her hair was short, with tight curls, and her eyes flashed big and white when she looked at you. She hadn't replied at first when Shimako spoke to her because she'd been too busy listening and responding to her phantom voices even to notice.

Now and then, as the roommate mumbled to herself, Shimako would hear her burst out laughing. Apparently she was sharing a joke with her illusory partner. At other times she would grow furious and start shouting. Again, it was the illusory partner she was angry with.

Shimako wrote a letter to her friend in Japan. She explained that, unfortunately, she'd been unable to continue the governess job she'd come here to do and was now in a mental institution.

A reply came. The friend didn't blame her for breaking the promise that had got her to America but was astonished to learn that Shimako was in a psychiatric hospital. What sort of illness is it, she wanted to know. Shimako herself didn't have a very clear understanding of her mental disorder. After all, not even the doctors ever gave very clear-cut explanations.

This hospital was a five-story building and had male patients as well. Word soon spread that a female Japanese had been admitted, and everyone wanted to talk to her.

She'd pass someone in the hall, and they'd say:
"Where are you from? Tokyo? That's wonderful!" Hoping to get her to stop and talk some more.

Meals were always noisy, clamorous affairs in the packed dining room. Shimako was too afraid of people to join the others. She would wait until they were finished and then slip in to eat. Her roommate often forgot about mealtimes, involved as she was with her hallucinations, so the nurse would come to get her.

After eating, Shimako was walking in the garden, as was another patient, an American man. She sat down beside him on a bench.

The first words Shimako said to him were:
"If you have a dollar, please give it to me."

She hadn't had any money of her own for a long time.

The man took five dollars from his pocket and handed it to her.

"Five dollars? Thank you! For two months I haven't had even a single dollar. You can't do anything without money."

Shimako ran to the gift shop, bought a chocolate bar, and returned to the bench, where the American was still sitting.

"Tell me," she said, "why are you here?"
"Depression. Sometimes I want to kill myself. I was

going to Columbia, but I asked for a leave of absence from school."

Oh, so he's a student, thought Shimako.

"What are you in for?" he asked.

"I hear voices, and I see things. I feel like I'm going crazy. May I ask your name?"

"Neil."

"Neil, will you be my friend? I don't have any friends, and I'm lonely. I came here from Tokyo about a year ago. I was working at different places, but it didn't go so well because of my illness. That's why I'm here."

There were about two hundred patients in the hospital. More women than men.

The grounds were covered with flower beds. Crocuses, gladioluses, and cannas were in bloom. The problem was that when Shimako looked at them, they became the raw material of hallucinations.

From behind, the cannas looked like the bodies of women.

The tips of gladioluses would elongate endlessly. Clusters of buds would telescope outward, tapering from the largest to the smallest, the ones on the tips getting infinitely smaller and narrower.

Mr. and Mrs. Hijikata, from the farm in New Jersey, came to visit.

"Missus," Shimako said, "please lend me a dollar if you have one. I haven't worked since I saw you, and I've been penniless all this time."

It had taken her only a week to use up the five dollars she'd got from the American.

Mrs. Hijikata felt sorry for her and gave her ten dollars.

"Missus, I still have dreams about working on the

farm. When I get better, please let me work for you again. I'll pay you back this ten dollars then."

Shimako was so dejected that this was all she could bring herself to say.

As luck would have it, Dr. Takeyama was also at the hospital that day.

"Hello there!" he said to the Hijikatas. "What a coincidence! How have you been? Thank you for coming to see Shimako. She tells me you lent her ten dollars. Which reminds me, Shimako, if you can find any part-time work here, I have no objections. I'll talk it over with the director of the clinic."

As it turned out, she was given permission to take a job washing dishes in the clinic's kitchen—but for no more than two hours a day. Shimako was happy with even that, however. After all, it provided her with pocket money.

Neil, the American who'd given her five dollars, was a student in the philosophy department of Columbia University. Shimako and he soon became good friends. Neil was a Japanophile who longed especially to visit Tokyo. He sometimes bought Shimako chocolates, which she loved.

Little by little Shimako's affection for Neil increased.

She felt truly lucky to have found such a good person in a place as vast as New York.

New York was the sort of place where it was not terribly unusual to fall in with a bad person who'd end up selling you as a prostitute. The city had it all: murder, drugs, violence, robbery—and with a little misfortune, anyone could stumble into trouble.

Shimako was extremely fortunate to be

recuperating in such a good hospital. She was ill in a foreign country. Impoverished, in the worst possible circumstances. She could never have imagined, while still in Japan, that she would ever reach such a state.

America was a big and complex country. That's why there were so many different sorts of people here.

Even people who were unbelievably kind.

Neil wore the gloomy expression typical of depressives. His shoulders were hunched and his eyes were empty. His cheeks were pale, like those of someone who was utterly without hope. Apparently he took a lot of antidepressants: he was forever complaining of a dry mouth.

Summer was slowly coming to an end. Even the huge leaves of the cannas in the garden were drooping. Their corollas yellowed, and the tips of them shriveled. The flowers withered and lost color each day. In the twilight, they looked like people on the verge of death. They might have been a parade of skeletons.

Looking out at them through the glass door one night, Shimako became convinced that the skeletons were walking toward her. She suddenly let out a great scream and hit the glass with her slipper, cracking it.

A startled nurse came on the run.

Shimako was crying and wailing. They're coming, the skeletons are coming, she screamed.

"No they aren't," the nurse said, trying to calm her. "Those are just dried-up old canna plants."

Shimako's black roommate took no notice of this incident but continued to concentrate on her imaginary conversation. To her, nothing that happened in the exterior world was of any importance.

When Shimako wanted to talk with her, she had to

tap her shoulder to get her attention; otherwise she'd merely remain absorbed in delusions. It was easier to handle this sort of friend and roommate, however, than it would have been were she a hyperactive manic patient.

When Neil was down he looked so despondent that it was painful to see him.

No matter what you did to try to cheer him up, it was useless. When he was depressed he hated even to speak. He wouldn't eat, either, but stayed shut up in his room. If he refused to eat for long periods, they'd have to feed him intravenously. Otherwise he'd be in danger of malnutrition.

"What's wrong, Neil? Cheer up."

He didn't want to hear words like this and found it bothersome even to be face to face with others. He'd merely maintain a grim and tight-lipped silence. It didn't matter who was trying to lift his spirits, at times like this it was hopeless. All he did was get more and more depressed and pessimistic.

The one thing Neil said all the time was:

"I want to die, I just wanna die. I want to kill myself."

But there was no discernible basis for these feelings. He simply wanted to die, for no apparent reason.

Some people, on the other hand, suffered from what was called "masked" depression. They would normally act as if nothing were wrong but then suddenly commit suicide.

One evening Shimako found Neil sitting on a bench in the garden and sat down next to him.

"Neil, how long have you had this illness?" she said.

"Since I was fifteen or sixteen, during puberty, when my parents divorced. I started locking myself in my room and just lay around wishing I could die—everything felt so dreary. I somehow managed to get into Columbia, but then in my first year I tried to kill myself."

He showed her his neck. There were three knife scars there. They were rounded and swollen-looking, having healed into ugly cords. In the summer, you'd be able to see them above a T-shirt. Shimako hadn't noticed because he wore turtlenecks all the time.

"You don't mess around, do you, Neil. That must have hurt. Why did you do it?"

"I didn't know what I was doing. Not till after I'd already done it. This is my second time in the hospital since then. How come you're here, Shima?"

He called Shimako "Shima." So did everyone else at the hospital.

"Me? My parents back in Japan never got along and were always fighting. And my oldest brother was an alcoholic, and a mean drunk, and he'd hit me and tease me.

"Ever since that time, I started feeling strange, at first like people were moving off far away from me, like a white curtain came down and cut me off from the outside world. Then it got so I couldn't make any sense out of what people were saying. They all got far, far away, and didn't seem to have any connection to me. The doctor called it depersonalization disorder, but after a while I started hearing voices and seeing things. You know, hallucinations.

"I was working on a farm in New Jersey, but then I got worse and the farmer and my doctor took me to a hospital. It was a horrible place. Like the insane asylums you see in movies. My doctor was afraid it would only make me worse. That's how I ended up coming here. And meeting you.

"You're twenty-five, Neil? So you're the same age as me. Let's be good friends, OK? I hope you get better soon. I think your illness is probably easier to fix than mine."

To which Neil replied:

"Not much difference in any case—illness is illness. And you can't know what it's like unless you've been through it yourself."

The loneliness of hospital life was starting to get to Shimako. Still, she thought, it beat being in her own home. The way she saw it, she was better off for just having escaped the family and all its problems.

A large number of the patients in this hospital were suffering from depression. Manic patients stood out because of all the noise they made, but those who were manic-depressive would undergo such drastic changes that they seemed like different people entirely. There were also patients with senile dementia, and others who suffered from epilepsy. Then there were the adolescent girls with anorexia. They were little more than skin and bone, and the first step in their treatment was always intravenous feeding.

A skilled doctor could take a manic-depressive and, by balancing the medicine with all the caution of a tightrope walker, suppress the manic and elevate the depressive tendencies to the point where the patient seemed like a normal person.

Schizophrenia, like Shimako had, was the most difficult illness to manage. Still not fully understood, it was a disease without an established and reliable treatment.

There was medication to counteract the auditory and visual hallucinations, but though it suppressed delusions it also reduced one's ability to think clearly, robbing one of the subtle faculties necessary to read, for example. Difficult things like books became incomprehensible.

That was the drawback. And it took at least three months to get back to your normal state even after you stopped taking the medicine.

Though this was too good a hospital to have impoverished patients, money and possessions were often stolen.

Whenever a patient was caught shoplifting at the nearby supermarket, the police would call the hospital, and a doctor would go to get him released.

"Not you again," the doctor would say. Manic patients, in their more excitable phases, would go into a supermarket and pocket everything they could lay their hands on. The police worked in conjunction with the hospital staff. They'd telephone, saying, "It's one of your patients again," and a doctor would hurry down to apologize and retrieve the culprit.

Foodstuffs from the hospital's common icebox were stolen regularly. Someone's strawberry jam would go missing, ice cream would vanish ... In a manic phase people grew outrageously bold and would help themselves to anything, regardless of whom it belonged to. They lost all sense of right or wrong, and the ability to distinguish others' possessions from their own.

Throughout the hospital, all sorts of things got stolen. Food was the most common, but belts, socks, even cheap articles of underwear hung out to dry after washing, were often targeted.

"Shima, you leave your underwear there and it'll disappear. Didn't you know? They'll steal all your panties and everything."

No wonder I seem short of undergarments lately, thought Shimako. Someone's been stealing them.

Now that she knew this, she began drying her clothes in her room, not in the common laundry. When she asked others, she learned that they'd been doing that all along.

Even coffee cups were fair game. And if you accidentally left your spoon in the dining room, it would soon be gone. The work of the manic banditos.

There was also a "boss" among the male patients who controlled the television channel, so that the women could never watch the shows they liked. The men's lobby had its own TV, but he nonetheless came to the women's just to throw his weight around. Not much could be done about it, of course, since the man was mad.

Any number of patients in this hospital thought nothing of causing problems for others. They were all disturbed people, after all.

At meals, Neil looked so dejected that one couldn't

help feeling sorry for him. He had no appetite, apparently, and left most of his food to be thrown away.

Shimako didn't have much of an appetite either. She felt constantly restless—standing up, sitting back down, standing back up again ...

Two or three other patients remarked how skittish she was.

"Shima, will you loan me a knife?" someone once asked, but Shimako had had all sharp objects taken away from her. Just to peel an apple, she was obliged to go all the way to the nurses' station and borrow a knife.

This was one of many little things that were inconvenient about living in a mental hospital. And Shimako was the only patient who'd entered this place without a dollar to her name. The others had families or guardians who gave them allowances. The money was held at the nurses' station, and each patient was allowed up to five dollars a day to use as he or she liked. Not more than that, though.

It was said that in an agitated state one patient, a middle-aged businessman who'd been admitted for mania, had spent four thousand dollars in a single day. He'd taken ten friends to an expensive restaurant and treated them to a lavish feast. An even more extreme manic case had once purchased four Cadillacs. One of the doctors had negotiated with the dealership to take the cars back. The patient had no need for four, he'd explained.

Neil was affectionately solicitous of his "Shima," but frowned when she told him about her hallucinations.

"That means it's schizophrenia," he told her.

Shimako felt that her illness was worse now than in her teens, when she'd begun to suffer from depersonalization. She hadn't had many hallucinations as a teenager. Now they were incessant.

"If you didn't have this disease, Shima, you'd be just about perfect," Neil said. "You're beautiful, and good-natured ..."

Shimako really was beautiful. Her black hair draped over her shoulders, and her big, dark eyes sparkled. As far as appearances went, she was a dream. It was unthinkable that a girl like her could have such an illness.

Neil often came to her room to visit, though this was actually against the rules. Men weren't allowed in the women's quarters. He had to sneak past the nurses to get there.

Shimako had not yet been given permission to leave the grounds. Neither had Neil. They'd promised to go to Central Park in New York together if they did get permission. And Neil said he'd also take her to his apartment near the park.

She'd managed to save some pocket money by working two hours a day. That kept her from sinking so low as to have to cadge things from others.

Shimako could not shake a feeling that Neil would commit suicide at some point.

"You'll see," he repeatedly declared. "Sooner or later I'll do myself in."

She sympathized with him. And she had little doubt that he would, indeed, choose to die one of these days. She could see it coming.

About once a year a patient at this hospital would

rip up his sheets, tie them to the wire mesh that covered the windows, and hang himself.

What's more, in the twenty-five years since the hospital had opened, sixteen patients had leaped from the roof of a fourteen-story apartment building in the neighborhood. The residents of the building had taken a tough stance against the hospital.

We want you to stop leaping off our roof and committing suicide, they demanded—otherwise we'll organize the residents to call for the removal of the hospital from this neighborhood. These demands angered the director of the hospital.

A number of celebrities and journalists lived in the apartment building. Perhaps the most unyielding of them all was a reporter for the weekly magazine *New York* named Ben Thurley.

It was said that after the last suicide, a girl of eighteen, the director had been summoned to the apartment building and forced to apologize in person.

But part of the blame lay in the building itself. The stairwell to the roof was left open, and it was easy for anyone to get up there. The issue was finally settled with an agreement to seal off the entrance to this stairwell.

Shimako had wondered if Neil might not climb that open stairwell and leap to his death, so she was happy when the entrance was closed. After that, there were no more suicides at the apartment building.

Neil helped to comfort Shimako's lonely heart. But anxiety kept that heart of hers in constant turmoil. With her illness she caused no end of problems for the nurses, yet she was forever dreaming of going back to work on the farm in New Jersey.

Once you developed schizophrenia, you might go years without getting better, however. Shimako was in no condition to hold a job out in the real world. Dr. Takeyama would never allow it.

It was all she could do just to get by inside the hospital.

Shimako gradually grew accustomed to America and Americans. And to the hospital as well.

The most beautiful part of the day was when sunset painted the hospital windows. The setting sun shone through the gaps in the craglike skyline of Manhattan and dyed the tops of the trees in the hospital garden red. The red dye spilled over to color even the clouds in the sky.

They were cumulonimbus clouds, and it took a long time for them to melt into the darkness.

The last glittering rays of the sun crawled over the flowers in the flower beds. The shriveling purple and pink petunias were bathed in the evening light, their velvet petals emitting a thick, glossy sheen. Those petals were beautiful to look at from any angle.

Shimako was sitting on the blue bench when Neil came along.

"Shima, how you feeling today? It's great that you finally got a part-time job, eh? Anytime you need more money, though, feel free to ask me. I'll be glad to help you in any way I can."

"I want to go back to New Jersey soon and work there," she said. "I'm in no position to stay on much longer in such an excellent hospital. I have to work. But I doubt if the doctor will let me yet."

"There's no need to be so impatient, Shima. Take as long as you need to recuperate. Some things in life you just can't rush. Remember, you've got me on your side here. Any time you have a problem, I'll help you out. Personal problems, I mean. Not that I think you'll have many problems—this hospital is a good place. Me, I can't go home till they release me. The doctor seems to think it would be dangerous to send me out into society right now. I guess he thinks I'll hang myself or something. And the truth is, my mind's so messed up that I myself don't know what I might do. But when I'm feeling good, I feel incredibly good."

Depression was a difficult illness to manage. A man could completely lose the energy to do anything, even wash his face.

Recently Shimako had, at long last, got to the point where on some days she could forget about the wounds her family had inflicted on her heart. It occurred to her that a whole year had already passed since she'd come to America. She was finally getting accustomed to her surroundings. And little by little her anxiety was easing.

She was also making more friends. They were a motley bunch, who suffered from drug addiction, mania, depression, manic-depression, senility—and when they gathered together the conversation tended to fly off every which way. Neil was practically normal compared to the rest of them.

Once summer passed and autumn came, the pampas grass on either side of the flower beds bloomed and rippled in the wind. Shimako approached and touched them. They were like delicate plumes of smoke.

There had been a riverbed covered with pampas grass behind her house in Japan.

But memories of home caused her distress; she felt

not the slightest desire to return there. Remembering her eldest brother, Yoshikichi, in particular, made her shudder. She could never forgive him for tormenting his own little sister as an outlet for all his frustrations.

The wisest course of action was to resign herself to the fact that she'd been born in a bad environment, and to let it all go now. She never intended to see any of them again.

She was sitting on the bench at the top of the slope, in a gloomy frame of mind, when Neil came along and sat down beside her. Neil, for his part, must have been feeling rather well; he was wearing a more cheerful expression than usual.

As Shimako gazed off into the distance, he reached over and fixed a stray lock of her hair. She gave a start. She couldn't remember a man ever doing anything like that for her before.

She was too embarrassed even to look Neil in the eyes.

"You seem in kind of a good mood today, Neil," she said, but he didn't reply. Then:

"Do you have a lover, Shima?" he asked.

"That's the least of my worries," she said.

During her year in America, bouncing about from place to place, finding a lover had been the furthest thing from her mind.

"I ask because, see, I find myself strangely attracted to you. That's one of the things that's making me so miserable. How do you feel about me?"

To be asked such a question out of the blue left her quite at a loss for an answer.

"Well, I haven't really thought about it," she said. "Are you in love with me?"

When she asked him this, Neil clammed up for some reason and peered off into the distance. Then he bowed his head and stared at the grass at his feet. In the end, Shimako had no way of knowing what his true feelings for her were.

Two or three days later a white envelope was lying on the desk in Shimako's room. She opened it, wondering who'd left it there. Inside was a poem.

Ailing, you journeyed from a distant land
With no means of healing your loneliness
When plumes of pampas grass dance in the air
Whitely blocking your view
What is it you think of?
That's what I long to know
If those thoughts can find life in this heart of mine
I'll gladly make room for them

Your Neil

How was she to reply?

Shimako was utterly nonplused. It was the first time in her life she'd received a love letter from a man.

From then on when she saw Neil she felt ashamed and avoided meeting his gaze.

Shimako liked Neil too. But what could possibly come of two individuals with so little in the way of prospects for the future, and in a place like this, harboring feelings of love?

Such was her less-than-optimistic view. She even wondered if someone like herself had any right to fall in love.

Shimako found the position she was in unbearably

sad. There was no telling when, if ever, she might be cured of her illness. What's more, she was alone, without any family at all in this vast country, America. She was barely managing to survive here, and wouldn't even be doing that if it weren't for the kindness of others. Twice she'd had to change jobs already. It made her feel pathetic.

It was really only because of her own feelings of inferiority that she didn't answer Neil's letter. She believed that if she were healthy and self-sufficient she would have accepted Neil's love.

The day after she'd received the letter she sat on the blue bench, and in a while Neil came along and sheepishly asked:

"Did you read my letter?"

"Yes, I read it," was all Shimako said.

In her heart of hearts, she liked Neil too. She just didn't know what to say, couldn't find the right words.

No more was said that day. Neil wore a look of despair.

Two days later another letter lay on her desk. The envelope was the same, so she knew it was probably from Neil. Shimako considered throwing it away at first, but finally opened it.

> *The autumn sky is not only blue*
> *But breathes white clouds and smoke*
> *Whose heart is it, I ask*
> *That has come to breathe in my heart?*
> *I will wait any number of days,*
>   *any number of years*
> *For that touch, fresh as a white cloud*
> *To give my heart a sign—I'm waiting*

Shimako was reluctant to sit on the blue bench again and shut herself in her room for several days.

When she ran into Neil in the dining room one evening, she kept her eyes lowered. She intentionally avoided meeting his gaze. The next day, as she was walking in the garden, Neil joined her and strolled along at her side.

Shimako spoke first.

"Thanks for the two letters. But even if I answered them, there would still be a wall between us that no one can do anything about. I'm a sick person. I don't want to cause you any trouble. I'm not in any position to go falling in love like some child. My future is jet black. I'm at a point where I don't know if I'll be able to go on living a regular life or end up a beggar. I'm only able to stay here because other people have shown me so much compassion. I want to work, but I couldn't get a job if I tried. The only job I can handle is washing dishes here for two hours a day. If you fell in love with me, I'd just cause you grief. So, as things stand, what good is it to know how you feel about me? What can I do about it?"

"You're being overly pessimistic," Neil said. "Who says sick people can't fall in love? You're too analytical, Shima. Don't think so much."

Shimako agonized. If this illness was just going to keep gnawing away at her forever, she had little hope for happiness in the future. When, if ever, might she be cured?

The next time Dr. Takeyama came to visit, she asked him.

"Doctor, is my illness incurable? Please tell me the truth. I need to know, or I won't be able to plan my future. I suppose schizophrenia is the worst of these sorts of illnesses, isn't it? There's probably no hope of ever being cured, right?"

"You must live each day believing that you can be cured," the doctor replied. "You have to control the illness, not fight with it. Growing impatient is of no help whatsoever."

Though her body might somehow manage to adapt to the medication that suppressed her hallucinations, the drug decreased her mental acuity to the point where she couldn't so much as write a letter. It clouded her brain. No one had yet come up with a medicine that was just right. Schizophrenia was basically a lifetime malady. Which was why Dr. Takeyama had been unable to offer any more than this in the way of an answer.

She'd probably be confined to hospitals her entire life. In which case, she had to come up with a suitable plan for herself. But the only plan she could think of was to commit suicide.

After all, it was ludicrous, wasn't it, to let human trash like her live a full span of life?

The next day she was sitting on the blue bench when, sure enough, along came Neil. The reason he always appeared when she was sitting there was that he could see the bench from his room on the second floor. All he had to do was look outside and he'd know whether or not she was there.

Neil sensed immediately that Shimako was depressed.

"What happened? You saw the doctor, and … ?"

"I think my illness is incurable. So, rather than

burdening people with my sickness, I'm seriously thinking it would be better to kill myself and have done with it."

"Kill yourself? You mustn't think about things like that, Shima."

What was with this person, anyway? He was the one who was always saying he was going to do himself in, but when Shimako said the same thing he told her she mustn't.

"Shima, if you commit suicide I won't have anything to live for. That's how deeply in love I am," he said, verbalizing his true feelings for the first time.

Neil claimed he was so in love with Shimako that he didn't see her illness as a problem. Surprised at these words, Shimako peered at his face, wondering if there could really be men like this in the world.

"I'd be willing to look after you, illness and all, for the rest of my life."

"You may think so now, but you'd be fed up with it after a month," she said. In her heart, she was still convinced that she couldn't rely on anyone.

Would she be in this hospital the rest of her life? She was now taking a smaller dosage of the medicine that controlled her hallucinations, but if she stopped taking it altogether she'd be right back where she started.

There wasn't a farm in all of New Jersey that would employ anyone in Shimako's condition.

And as she sat gazing idly at the clouds in the lingering light of dusk, she knew that not even in the most remote corner of her heart was there any desire to return to Japan. Not that unhappy memories of home still haunted her all that much. Her present agonies so weighed upon her that she could scarcely think of anything else.

There was no way out. If she could just get rid of the hallucinations, she'd like to go to work somewhere. Perhaps the hospital would employ her on a long-term basis. That was her only thread of hope.

Thoughts of Neil flitted through her heart from time to time, but it was not as if she were passionately in love with him. Love was more of an extravagance than Shimako's heart had room for.

Far from being able to accommodate such feelings, she was completely occupied with worries about the future—and concern for her present predicament.

Rack her brains as she might, she could come up with no great plans. The origin of her problems, however she looked at it, lay in her illness. Would this illness weigh upon her for most of her life—or, worse, forever?

When she asked Dr. Takeyama such questions, he always answered in the same ambiguous way. It was just the same old advice over and over again.

She heaved a deep sigh. Was her illness incurable? That was the question it always came back to. When she thought about these things, her sorrow expanded to fill her entire heart.

The sky was growing dark. As she strolled over the lawn, the wind passed beneath the plumes of pampas grass and dislodged a wisp that had caught in her hair. It was already too dark to remain outside; she'd have to return to her room.

She had climbed halfway up the slope when she

suddenly sensed someone near and gave a start.

"Oh, it's you, Neil. What are you doing here now? It's late."

"I was standing here watching you. You're so beautiful, such an Oriental beauty, it's hard to believe you're ill. Didn't my poem touch your heart at all? If not, I'll lose all hope."

"It isn't that. I'm staying away from you because I'm sick. Don't you see? If I were healthy, believe me, I wouldn't hesitate to leap into your arms. You understand, don't you? I can't become your girlfriend if I'm only going to cause you grief. I have feelings for you, too. After all, I'm in the prime of life myself. But my situation is just too hopeless. I'm not qualified to talk about love. Love has to be a much healthier thing—that's what I think.

"You should choose someone in better health, Neil. Your illness isn't that serious. You're not much different from everyone else, as long as you take your medicine. But my mind is so disturbed that I can hardly even control myself. It's all I can do to get through each day. I don't have room in my heart to think about love and such. Can you understand that?"

It was now pitch dark outside.

Light leaked from the hospital windows and cast a faint glow on the green grass below.

Before she realized it, Shimako was climbing the slope hand in hand with Neil.

"I don't think there's anything wrong with falling in love when you're recuperating from an illness, Shima," Neil said as they parted. "I'll wait for you, forever."

But Shimako truly wasn't in any condition to fall in love. Even when she took her medicine she still suffered auditory hallucinations. There were times when she would attack a nurse, mistaking her for one of the people in her delusions. She even hit the black girl with whom she shared a room, thinking it was her voice she was hearing.

Neil didn't know about incidents like these.

Shimako pulled some sort of stunt each day. Her illness didn't appear to be getting any better at all.

She herself, of course, had no idea if she was getting better or getting worse. She was constantly preoccupied with her struggle. Even at her part-time job washing dishes, she took nearly as many days off as she worked.

She could only work during times when she had a certain emotional equilibrium. Otherwise she was likely to startle the others by breaking dishes, at which point her supervisor would call her over and say:

"Why don't you take the day off?"

Autumn too was slipping away, having dried up the flowers in their beds. Frost covered them now, and snow began to fall.

The snowbound slope made for dreary scenery. Sunlight grew weaker, and when sleet fell, the snow would end up with a coating of ice. The slope was slippery then, and dangerous to walk on.

Even the cars needed tire chains.

To Shimako it seemed that all the people living outside the hospital must be happy.

A great loneliness had arisen from the depths of her heart. Sick in a foreign country, with no family, relying on new acquaintances. Unable to work.

Dr. Takeyama happened to come by one day as she

was agonizing over her plight. She showed him a sketchbook in which she'd drawn some of her hallucinations.

"These are the sorts of things I see, Doctor."

"It must be exhausting to have such things constantly appearing before your eyes," he said.

In the sketchbook was a drawing of Dr. Kearn surrounded by innumerable white spots, like drops of water, in which his right arm appeared to trace perhaps a hundred separate lines. There was a drawing of the striped pattern on her bed twisting and bulging upwards, and one of countless gravestones lining the slope. When the doctor saw a drawing of balloonlike objects floating in rows in midair, completely filling the field of vision, and another of countless bones scattered about, he asked if she wanted him to prescribe more medication.

"But, Doctor, even if you gave me more medicine it would only be a temporary solution, right? I want to get out and go to work. I'd like to work on that farm in New Jersey and support myself. I want to earn my own way somehow, but I can't even do a proper job as a dishwasher here in the hospital. I end up breaking dishes. It's hopeless.

"But, anyway, I wanted to show you something, Doctor. Look at these letters I got from my friend Neil."

Shimako showed him the two poems. Dr. Takeyama was taken aback when he read them.

"If you have such a splendid friend you shouldn't hesitate to spend time with him, to dispel the gloomy hospital atmosphere. I'm all for this friend of yours," he said, then added:

"Having a man who loves you might change your luck. You say he's willing to help you with your illness for the rest of his life? He sounds like a faithful and sincere person to me. I'd like to meet this Neil. Is that all right with you?"

The doctor went off to find Neil's room. In about thirty minutes he returned and said to Shimako:

"He's a very serious young man. And all he suffers from is relatively minor depression. He seems to be very much in love with you. I don't think you could ask for a better boyfriend. What do you think, Shimako? How do you feel about him?"

"I don't dislike him, but I'm so busy struggling with my illness every day that I don't really have time for love. It would be all right if my symptoms lessened, but I'm overwhelmed each day with hallucinations. I don't have a chance even to think about Neil very much."

"Thinking about Neil might ease your symptoms and direct your thoughts toward him all the more. I recommend you spend time with him. Few men are as gentle and kind as he seems to be. He shows a good understanding of your illness, as well. Not many people in this world are capable of understanding an illness like yours. That alone is something to be grateful for."

The sunlight of early spring shone on the slope.

Between the patches of snow, crocuses, hyacinths, and tulips sprouted, splitting the black earth. Some of the sprouts were quite large and had even formed flower buds.

The firm, plump buds that would soon be pale pink hyacinths grew larger each day as they absorbed the sunlight of spring.

The buds on the willow trees halfway up the slope were swollen too. Their silver tips swayed softly in the wind.

People were relieved that the frigid winter was gone. Winters in New York were severely cold. Liberated from the daily trial by snow, everyone began to look hopefully forward to spring.

The snow and ice on the slope melted, so that people could stroll upon it again.

Shimako was happy that spring had come. Thinking about her illness depressed her, but the vitality of spring filled the surroundings with tangible joy.

She saw a lot of Neil on days like this.

With the advent of spring and the chance to use the slope again, the two of them often went out walking.

Though Neil's parents had divorced, both of them resided in New York and came separately to visit him. His father owned a company that manufactured duralumin. He visited once a week. Neil was to take over the business after his father, who was therefore especially worried about him.

Neil's mother was a gentle, quiet woman.

They'd divorced because the father had found himself a lover. A woman younger than Neil, no less.

Neil had his father's classical, well chiseled features and was quite tall. When Shimako walked beside him she barely came up to his shoulder.

She now had a deep affection for him. Aside from her doctors, no one she'd met had been this nice to her since she'd arrived in America. His kindheartedness is what won her over.

Knowing that Shimako had no money, Neil often

procured various things for her in the city. During winter, when he'd learned she didn't own a winter wrap, he'd bought her a beautiful long black coat as a gift.

But how much of what she felt was love and how much just friendship, not even she herself really knew. When it came to things of this sort, one might say she was still very much a child.

Neil sat on the newly sprouted grass atop the slope, his eyelashes glittering white in the sunlight. His skin was so pale as to seem almost transparent, and the warmth of the spring sun caused his cheeks to flush pink.

Shimako sat beside him, squinting in the light to gaze steadily at his profile.

Each day her fondness for him grew.

Of late, she could hardly get through the day without Neil. He gave her pocket money, caramels, chewing gum ... He also treated her to dinners at the restaurant across from the hospital. The hospital food was terrible.

And even though they saw each other every day, he still sent her love letters.

He lavished all his kindness on Shimako. This was helping to ease the anxiety and isolation she felt in America.

Even her habitual loneliness was fading.

"Neil ... I'd like to go out and find a job somewhere. What do you think? I still don't have much confidence. I am somewhat more accustomed to my job here, washing dishes, but ... If I want to get something better, the only place I can go is that farm in New Jersey. The Hijikatas treat me like a member of the family, so even if I made a mistake I don't think they'd yell at me. When I was working there before they seemed to really like me, you know. I'm a good worker. But I quit because of my illness. If I hadn't got sick, I bet I'd still be there, working like mad. I want to go back."

Neil made every effort to dissuade her.

"I don't see why you have to get yourself some job all of a sudden," he said. "I think you should take your time, stay right here for now. I'll see to it that you have everything you need. You don't have to go to work. Let's keep on just as we are, recuperating in this nice, peaceful environment. If you run off somewhere now, you'll just end up coming back here. It's not as if you're really cured, after all. You don't think you're cured, do you? You mustn't leave the hospital yet. I'll do everything I can for you. Take your time."

The truth is that Shimako didn't know if she was getting better or not. But she knew that illnesses like hers lasted a long time. There was little chance of her having been cured already.

No, she could hardly consider herself cured when she still suffered hallucinations.

One day Neil told her of something he'd heard.

It seemed there was a hospital where one could work while receiving treatment. They had a new system in which patients who were artists could paint, for example, or musicians could study and practice their art while remaining hospitalized.

Shimako wanted to go there, and Neil said he'd like to go with her. It was in Connecticut, he said. On land with groves and woods and ponds.

They went as soon as they'd got permission from Dr. Takeyama. Shimako was astonished at what they saw. There were even fields where the patients grew vegetables.

The patients received hourly wages for their work each day. Those who wanted to paint pictures spent the entire day painting. And there was a channel through which the paintings were sold in New York.

Shimako clutched Neil's hand in excitement. To earn money while receiving treatment—this was a once-in-a-lifetime opportunity, and she wasn't going to let it slip away.

Her first week there, Dr. Takeyama came to see her and was pleasantly surprised to find that, if anything, the place exceeded his expectations.

"This is a new concept in hospitals," he said enthusiastically. "It's ideal. We mustn't just feed patients medication and put them to bed. I think it's much better for them to work and slowly make their way back into society."

A nurse was in charge of the vegetable fields. Shimako felt she wouldn't mind working there the rest of her life. They grew cabbages, tomatoes, eggplants, and so on—many of which were prepared in the kitchen and served to the patients.

She went with Neil to look at the ward where patients painted pictures. The hospital supplied the artists with paints with which to create their masterpieces. It was said that the director of the hospital was a painter himself, and a specialist in art therapy.

One day all the patients in the hospital gathered in the atelier to try their hands at painting. The works were later displayed in a hall in New York. The exhibition was entitled "Pathological Expression."

In one classroom patients shaped clay into pottery all day. They made plates and teacups and teapots and vases. These were sold at church-related charity organizations and art shops in New York. Painted, they were joyous, colorful works that evoked an atmosphere of freedom.

There was even a fashion department. Two specialists came from New York to serve as instructors. The products of this department were mainly simple things that even patients could make, like aprons and skirts. These too were sold in New York.

The patients were self-sufficient, thanks to their daily wages, and many could pay their entire hospital bills themselves.

Shimako was delighted. Hope for the future, which she'd been without for so long, was reborn inside her. Even if hers was a lifelong, incurable illness, at least in this place she could work and earn her own way.

Several of the patients working there were schizophrenic. The nurses watched over them as they gave them instruction. Shimako felt as if the world had suddenly grown brighter right before her eyes.

Since entering the new hospital, Shimako was in better spirits each day. She no longer spent entire days in her room, submerged in thought, as she had before.

She pulled weeds and tended the vegetables devotedly. When she wasn't well she was allowed to stay out of the fields and rest.

The money she earned was enough to pay the extremely reasonable hospital bill. The rate was determined by how much each patient could pay. In Shimako's case, the discount was so considerable that her hourly wages covered it all.

A variety of things were for sale in the gift shop. All the merchandise was made by people in the hospital. There were cookies baked by patients, under the guidance of nurses, and handbags other patients had made. Also aprons and what have you, sewn in the dressmaking section.

There were even pickles that had been prepared by patients.

Shimako was deeply grateful to have made it to this place. Even if she were never cured of her illness, she thought, at least she'd be able to work. She couldn't have asked for a greater stroke of luck.

"Neil, I'm really just so happy to have come here. This place is perfect for me. I'm going to stay here the rest of my life, and never get married. Don't you think that's best? I doubt if I could ever make it outside of the hospital. I suffer too constantly from my illness, and I just don't think I could get by out there. There's no place for me in society, and I can't imagine living like everyone else. To have this colony to stay in is like a dream come true."

When she glanced at Neil, he was wearing a long face. Startled, Shimako asked why he was looking so sad. With tears welling up in his eyes, Neil finally choked out an answer:

"You say you're going to live here the rest of your life without a husband or a lover. I guess it's all right if I come to visit you sometimes?"

Shimako honestly hadn't understood why Neil had tears in his eyes. It now occurred to her that perhaps all this time he'd actually been hoping for a normal married life with her in the outside world.

If so, it was only natural that he'd be saddened by the sight of Shimako enthused about spending her life alone in the colony. She, in short, was being completely insensitive to his feelings.

Shimako wondered if, having been so badly abused as a child, she simply had no understanding of people's good will. Thinking about it, she realized it was only because of the kindness of others that she'd been able to leave the land of her birth and travel halfway around the world. Without that kindness she would never have made it this far.

Her first sponsor, who'd invited her to America and given her the job as a nanny. The Hijikatas. Dr. Takeyama. The rich American woman at the Japan Society, whom she still hadn't met. The kindly Dr. Kearn. And now the director of this colony.

More kindhearted people than she could count, and then, of course, there was Neil, her closest friend. Neil, who bought her candy and even gave her pocket money. The one who was at her side whenever she was lonely. The one who grieved and rejoiced with her.

Perhaps, Shimako thought, I'm a fortunate person after all. There's so much kindness in the world. I may suffer from this illness for the rest of my life, but maybe on my own I'll continue to meet all sorts of people who'll be willing to help me.

Up till now, she hadn't even considered marrying Neil and trying to steer her way through the world with him. No such thought had ever entered her mind. But Neil, sitting there with his eyes brimming with tears, felt differently. He wanted to live with Shimako all his life.

She, on the other hand, was convinced she could

be happy spending the rest of her days here in the colony, working.

Neil's illness was not that serious; he could live in society. Shimako, however, having already changed jobs a number of times, didn't believe she could live in the world like a normal person.

For her, marriage was about as tangible as the dream of a dream.

Neil felt so strongly about Shimako that he was willing to take responsibility for protecting her from the world. That could only be true of someone deeply in love.

But what was most frustrating for Neil, what tore up his heart, was that Shimako didn't even seem willing to try to let his love inside, or work with him to help it grow.

Here she was, going into raptures right before his eyes about being able to support herself for the rest of her life inside the colony. Did he cast such a thin shadow in her heart? Didn't she depend upon him at all?

Neil agonized. Though he wanted to help Shimako in her illness, she wanted to spend her life among a group of sick people sequestered from society. Apparently she thought very little of his love.

Shimako could not imagine that any man in this world would want to marry her, given her illness. Many people were kind to others. But to marry someone and try to struggle through life with them, that was something else entirely.

If Neil was thinking that far, he was too deeply committed to her. It would have been understandable if she were merely depressive. A little dysthymia wasn't such a problem. Or if she were simply neurotic—then a cure would be feasible. But he probably didn't really understand a disease as malignant as schizophrenia. He'd been with her only during "good" times, when she was taking medication. He wasn't really aware of how fearsome this illness was.

The colony was known as the Neuberger Foundation Treatment Center. The director was a Dr. Morris, chairman of the American branch of an art therapy movement.

The facilities included the farmland and a rehabilitation center. There were two hundred patients, but plenty of space. The grounds were a good ten times the size of those at the previous hospital.

Neil, who'd entered the colony with Shimako, stayed in the men's ward.

There were woods and a lake, and the fields were planted with all sorts of vegetables. In their free time, Neil and Shimako could stroll around as they liked.

There was also a library, a drafting studio, and a swimming pool.

Shimako's main doctor here was a man named Bruhms, who had once been a painter. That was before he'd gone to medical school. Intrigued by art therapy, he'd enrolled in a college that specialized in psychology. He'd done his internship at this colony and had now been a full member of the staff for five or six years.

He was also interested in Japan, and his interest only increased after he met Shimako. Unlike Neil, Dr. Bruhms was a specialist and well aware of how devastating an illness schizophrenia could be. But he too was utterly captivated by Shimako's beauty. If she weren't sick, he might very well have proposed to her. He so enjoyed and looked forward to his sessions with Shimako that such thoughts actually crossed his mind.

Dr. Bruhms had a good understanding of how painful Shimako's hallucinations were for her. Each time they began recurring he prescribed medication.

She would appear to be getting somewhat better, then suddenly have a bad relapse. Neil still maintained that whether her illness was curable or not, he was prepared to look after her. But the doctor felt that the disease would make normal married life impossible.

Neil's thinking betrayed his wealthy background. If someone in the family was sick, you hired a nurse. If Shimako was too ill to cook, he could have the maid do it.

The same was hardly true for the doctor, however. It would be disastrous for him if his wife couldn't cook. And he didn't have the money to hire a maid.

This is what Dr. Bruhms told Shimako:

"Shima, you should spend your life here in the colony. There's no sense in forcing yourself to return to society. You're certainly not up to living out there right now. You've already changed jobs twice, right? Why struggle to fit into society when you can stay with us?

"As long as I'm here I'll see to it that you're well taken care of. You like to paint pictures, right? So why not stay here and paint whatever you like? It's not impossible, Shima, that you could become established as an artist. Here at the colony you have paints, brushes, space, everything you need. I'll prepare a canvas for you tomorrow. Won't you try painting something?

"Or you could try to write novels, or poetry. This hospital is well known as a center for art therapy. Van Gogh, Munch—they too, of course, were mentally ill, but think of all they accomplished before their deaths. If you want me to, Shima, I'll help you develop your art. It's a good idea, don't you think? If you're interested, you won't have to labor like the others growing eggplants and tomatoes. I think you can make better use of your hospital life by specializing in art.

"Once you get enough works together and want to hold an exhibition, I'll negotiate for you with an art dealer in New York. I saw a drawing you left unfinished in the drafting studio, and I'd say you have real talent. Let's decide this today, Shima—you're going to be a painter. We can go right now and start setting up your atelier. The hospital will supply all the paints and canvases, so you can paint to your heart's content. Then you won't have to do manual labor like the others."

He even went so far as to add:

"You can train as an artist and let the world judge your talent. That way you'll be able to stay right here and still find your place in society."

Shimako loved the studio that was set aside for her. One of her more striking works was a large canvas upon which she painted a male figure. It was Neil. Dr. Bruhms saw it and asked:

"Who is this?"

"That's my closest friend, Neil. He's a very kind person who has always supported me."

"Do you love this fellow?" Dr. Bruhms asked abruptly.

"I don't know yet," said Shimako. This was true. She really didn't know if she loved Neil or not.

Shimako wasn't even aware that Dr. Bruhms was in love with her. And yet, if she weren't suffering from schizophrenia, Dr. Bruhms would probably have proposed marriage to her on the spot.

And Neil wanted to marry her, illness or no illness. As soon as he received permission to spend the night outside the hospital, or to leave altogether, he wanted to take Shimako home to his father. For this reason, he was eagerly awaiting the day he'd be released.

But he needed to persuade Shimako first. And because of her illness, Shimako was hesitating to commit to love.

Neil's release was finally approved.

"Shimako-san, the hospital has given me permission to leave. Let me take you with me to my father's house, and we'll get married. Then I'll hire a nurse and a maid to take care of you. What do you say?

"You and I can start a family, Shima. It's my fondest wish. Think about it—do you really want to spend the rest of your life in a hospital? If you never leave this colony, your life will have been a failure. People only become real human beings by living in the real world. Please make up your mind and come with me. I'll take responsibility for your illness. I'll protect you. I'll take responsibility for everything. Please come home with me."

"But, Neil, I'm sick. And with the worst kind of sickness—schizophrenia. I don't want to burden you with that. I love you, of course. But I can't marry anyone as long as I'm like this. It's my duty to let you go. I don't want to force my incurable illness on you. I can't just lightly accept an offer of marriage. It would make a complete mess of your life. There are as many healthy women as there are stars in the sky, and you should find yourself one of them. I want to stay in a place that's suited to someone with my condition. You understand."

With these words Shimako refused him. Everything she'd said was true. The more love she felt for Neil, the less she wanted to burden him with her problems.

"What I'm saying," she went on, "is that it's because I love you that I won't marry you. I don't want to tie you down. I want you to be free. Marry someone healthy and have healthy children. You can't hope for anything like that with me."

Neil was crushed. He threw his arms around Shimako and wept. His tears fell upon Shimako's hand.

But even after he was released from the hospital, Neil came to visit two or three times a week. He wasn't about to give up.

Under Dr. Bruhms's guidance, Shimako's painting made spectacular progress; she improved each day.

Soon she'd accumulated a great number of works. Not even Dr. Bruhms had imagined she would develop so quickly. He now thought she might very well end up an established artist in spite of her illness.

He brought an art critic friend of his, Bob Lindner, from New York for a second opinion. Lindner raved about the paintings and fervently pressed for a one-woman exhibition in New York.

The exhibition became a reality.

The *New York Times* printed a glowing review.

Neil showed up carrying a bouquet of flowers and full of enthusiasm for the artistry of the paintings.

"Shima, I never realized you had such tremendous talent. Maybe you can actually make it in the art world."

Dr. Bruhms declared that she would be able to support herself as an artist.

Every single one of the paintings sold.

Shimako wanted only to remain in the colony and refine her art.

At long last Shimako had a small measure of peace of mind.

She was certain in her heart that this was the life for her. Determined to become an established artist, she continued painting with even greater intensity. The "subjects" she painted were her hallucinations. It was small wonder that she caused such excitement on the New York art scene. Her paintings were truly unique.

Dr. Bruhms knew this better than anyone. He was convinced that Shimako's art was the real thing.

She painted what one might call landscapes of the heart. And they captured quite astonishingly the hallucinations peculiar to schizophrenics. No one else in the New York art world painted such pictures. They undeniably communicated a certain mysterious something to the viewer. Some people even began to suggest that she was a true genius.

After moving about from place to place, Shimako had at last found a situation that suited her and brought some serenity to her heart.

She was overjoyed with the pleasure of releasing through her paintings the torments her heart had harbored for so long.

Shimako believed she'd found the right path for herself. She was quite certain that this would be her life's work. She was prepared to dedicate herself wholeheartedly to painting, to let painting be her only real friend and salvation.

Both Neil and Dr. Bruhms delighted in and praised each new picture she painted. Their encouragement guided her toward recovery. Shimako grew steadily as an artist.

Her paintings came to exhibit an ever more startling originality. And even her illness took a turn for the better, thanks to the power of art. Whenever the hallucinations started up she would step to the easel and capture them in a painting.

Dr. Takeyama was very happy with the way things were turning out. He said this was the ideal lifestyle for Shimako.

death smell acacia

The white, waxlike petals were turning to transparent shells that adhered one by one to the sunlight pouring down from heaven to earth. The forest of acacia trees hung over Masao's head, a dome of thousands of blossoms. Earth's gravity tugged effortlessly at the near weightlessness of the white flowers as the petals melted in shimmering sunbeams that escorted them to the ground below. Masao watched the soft ivory clouds of early summer snagging on treetops then breaking free, entwining in branches then releasing and drifting away. The fragrance spilling out of the pistils permeated deep inside his lungs.

Though it had been a month since his wife's death he hadn't sent her body to the crematorium. He still had sex with the body each day. The oppressive, hideous stench of the corpse filled the house, a gray fetor of death that coated his lungs and that the fragrance of acacias did its best to dislodge.

From the roof of the house, beneath the branches, a ghostly, faint red ribbon of light rose stealthily heavenward. The soul of the departed had clung to the roof for days, and the tips of the copious flowers had already begun to wither amid the unwonted smell of rotting flesh. The withering had been especially pronounced these last few days. The weather had warmed with the advent of early summer, and the red inner folds of his wife's vagina had grown soft and bloated and begun to fall apart during copulation, like overripe fruit decomposing. The forest treetops gagged at the smell. When he inserted his penis in the decaying organ, the well of emotions held sway over his entire body. Those tender folds embraced his member just as they'd done when she was alive; it was wondrous how even as they decomposed they lost none of the resilience they'd had in life. It was as if, though the body was dead, the vagina alone continued to breathe.

 She'd died of uterine cancer. Near the end, as she grew ever weaker, her vagina had dripped with a foul-smelling discharge. He'd wiped it clean with towels and gauze. The discarded gauze had eventually come to form a great pile in the middle of the room. At night, in the moonlight that filtered through the window, the decaying bacteria in the gauze emitted a blue-white glow. Gazing at the strange glittering of the moonlit substance, Masao had sunk into the abyss of carnal desire. Pressing his dying wife's knees apart with his hands, he made love to her sexual organ. The white slime of his ejaculation could be seen clearly in the dim light, copulating with the cancer cells that spilled from her slit. Then it would drip to the floor and spread. Moonlight etched the edges of the expanding shape with glistening silver.

 Her death had come all too quietly.

 "What are you doing between my legs?" she'd

muttered, her consciousness growing ever hazier as the room waited in hushed silence to greet her soul's surrender.

But her sex organ alone lived on. A month had passed. Masao continued to sleep with the body.

He carried her out into the garden and turned her genitalia toward the sun to dry. Then, without warning, white acacia petals began to scatter to the ground with a noiseless fury, transforming it before his eyes into a world of silver-white. The petals covered her pubic mound as well. He disturbed that virginal white surface to clear with trembling hands only the area of her sex. From time to time the pink crack of her vagina changed hue in the shade of passing clouds. One torn fragment of cloud slipped between the folds of her slit, and something began to move beneath the bushy growth of her mound. The blood vessels deep inside there had solidified and turned purple. Ghostly sunlight coiled around her ruined veins and tried to wriggle its way deeper inside. The once supple blood vessels were now as hard and brittle as glass; as they absorbed the light they cracked and snapped audibly. Splintering.

The life of all flesh and blood is but a moment in time. An ephemeral, blooming silence in the boundless sea of eternity. It was difficult, of course, for Masao to accept the death of the wife he'd so doted upon. Memories of the days he'd buried his cheeks between her ample breasts. The colors of her summer clothes, swelling with sensual desire. Her sex, breathing soft in the shadow of pubic hair. An expansiveness like the surface of a honeyed lake, swallowing without a ripple all the love and desire of his youth. Days when those slender white fingers intertwined his own, days of whispered words of affection—days that were gone forever now. The black hair that once fell luxuriantly to her shoulders now reeked of death. In simmering waves of sunlight filtered through acacia blossoms, Masao lightly lifted the ends of that long black hair in his hands. The endless afternoons of darkness and grief, when he'd been unable even to choke down his food because of the sorrow that filled his breast, had passed; now all that remained of his heart was a vast emptiness. For the past month he'd closed himself up indoors with Mimiko's corpse. Thirty days of sleeping with a corpse, talking to a corpse, having sex with a corpse.

    Masao was afraid. Afraid the body might in time deteriorate so badly that it would fall to pieces. Mimiko would disappear from his vision. Cease to exist. He saw himself there, growing ever more fretful. His beloved wife decomposing. Broken fragments of the love with whom he'd shared brilliant youth lay voiceless, the sparkle gone from her eyes. Who was he fooling, carrying her corpse into the garden to dry her vagina in the sun? Slowly but surely all her love was perishing. He was losing her. His eyes pored over every detail of her body, from the tips of her toes to the ends of her hair. He never tired of looking at her. Days when her beauty had been in full bloom were already just scenes from dreamlike, distant memories; now her swollen flesh hung loosely from her bones. Her blood, pulseless and stagnant, lay in deep-purple pools that no longer reflected the sunlight. When he touched her bloated skin, shadows of that lifeless blood enveloped his hand, crawled up his arm, and spread over his entire body, dyeing it a ghostly purple hue. Softly his penis began to swell. The early summer sun was still entangled in the upper branches of acacia trees but had begun to decline westward. White liquid, translucent in the sunlight, gushed from the head of his penis. The semen penetrated the transparent highlands air and spurted over Mimiko's eyes, those eyes that would never blink again. And was then transformed into tiny, squirming, particulate clumps.

Amid insinuations of Eros an endless succession of maggots emerged from her eyes and crawled to the ground. Masao watched as his jism became a mass of worms wriggling in the dirt. He peered closer, tracing their path back to the cracks in the rotting flesh from which they continued to issue. The larvae multiplied and spread over the countless acacia petals stuck fast to the ground. The dormant petals began to move.

Maggots crawled up the black bark of acacias and swarmed to the tips of the uppermost twigs. As if to ascend to heaven.

With vacant eyes, Masao gazed up at what lay beyond love. Now all the treetops of the forest were festooned with semen. Dripping. Wriggling. He went pale with the momentary thought that youth, the youth he'd spent with Mimiko, had been only an illusion.

When, in the flower of her youth, cancer had attacked her womanhood itself, her reproductive organs, she'd said, as if in delirium:

"But even if I die now, I still feel fortunate—to have met someone like you. Passion is a fleeting thing, and only for the living."

Passion, the froth of love, lives only a moment in

the world of men. And at passion's end, smeared with the smell of death, worms devour the acacia forest of love.

Masao, pale with anxiety, peered at those squirming worms of death.

They twisted and writhed, leaving lustrous scars upon the overlapping clusters of acacia blossoms; the clusters, unable to support the weight, fell to earth along with their pliant, slimy burdens.

The larvae came down like scattered rain, falling upon the living and the dead. The edges of the acacia petals turned from ivory to sepia, their tips dried to the consistency of plastic. The plastic petals collided with audible clicks as they crowded upon the ground. Mimiko's earth-entombed soul would be resurrected amid a dazzling movement of flowers and maggots.

Masao gazed at her, watching, waiting.

Her eyes were locked on some distant scenery, a limpid lake-bottom blue at the end of space and time. He thought he saw the flesh beneath her jet-black eyebrows twitch. A faint flush of red arose on her blood-drained lips.

O petals that have come to call in the sleepless ravine between night and day. Scattering over the road to death, acacia blooms falling, piling up higher than the sky, petals by the tens of thousands to bury a youthful corpse more lonesome than a star and to still the blinking of glittering eyes. You're gone, up that path to the mound of silence, today and yesterday and tomorrow and the day after that, the flowers white, white, white, the final accumulation. The tomb of our unfulfilled phantom passion. O forest of love! Let the petals cover these scars of oblivion, at the end of our luckless bonds of affection. Enough to erase the wounded hole of the smell of death, the heart only aching more with the passage of days, festering, the hill of memory, crushing flowers underfoot, ending in passion, O woman I could have eaten alive! To end it all in the cleft of love, a knife to pierce our two red hearts like fruit. The numbing grief of the heart rent asunder. Let flowers scatter upon the fresh grave of excruciating pain, exhausted ash-colored youth. Faster than the dark terminus, faster than the sound of a blink, love merely shakes off the vaginal anguish and passes on. One day, suddenly, existence will dye our vision leopard-eye gray.

Though early summer has come, the blossoms are faded, broken, never again a young summer this lovely, a vision of you so distant it all but disappears, arriving only to leave us again, the unmelted snow of futile youth. Today the body shudders with the uncertainty of life. The fruitlessness of pursuit too fresh in the memory for passion to trample oblivious death and pass on at the edge of the highland forest. O destiny of unbearable love! The clouds in the distant sky are white, brilliant, no art can embrace them, gone in the morning, forming again in the sky, look up and chase them with the eyes, passion that vanishes in the night. It's love that lies in the layers of illusion, stepping on nothingness, wandering in the forest; and such is youth: a voyager set adrift, rowing the days away in delirium, or love and passion that merely pass through this decaying flesh, as if they were nothing at all.

O lost passion! The curtain of death has fallen.

O dead flesh, left behind in the cushion of stillness that stole our passion!

Leaving Mimiko's body among the flowers, Masao walked back to the veranda. Dust clung to his feet when he stepped on its wooden planks. Dispirited and dazed as he was, he'd done no cleaning, and as he moved through the house specks of debris rose up to coil about the legs of his jeans. He took the newspapers from the box each day, lest the man who delivered them grow suspicious, but then merely dropped them on the concrete floor of the entryway, where so many had now piled up he scarcely had room to walk.

Masao was a superrealist painter. To support himself he also worked part-time for an architectural firm. Superrealist works require a tremendous amount of time: he often took as long as three months to finish a single piece. Unless one weaved one's way through every mesh in the net of beauty—each individual hair, each nuance of eyebrow—the canvas would not come alive. He painted so that even the blood vessels could be faintly seen beneath the skin of hands. When he painted flowers, you could almost smell the narcissus petals on the canvas. And when he was finished, it was not unusual for the actual flowers he was painting to wither, as if the life had been drained from them.

Year in, year out, in a dimly lit room, he obeyed the inner fire, observing the stealthy shadows that played over wildflowers, women, purple butterflies, and seashells.

He'd met Mimiko at the art institute, where she modeled. She was just a poor girl in need of money, sent by a local agency. If she'd worked out of an agency in Tokyo she might have found a steady job modeling for a famous artist or a college of fine arts. But in a little highlands city like this, one was lucky to find a single school that required models.

She was poor, but Masao, too, was barely making ends meet. In his part-time job with the architectural firm he worked days at construction sites as an assistant to carpenters or laborers—strenuous, dirty work—and at night he studied at the only art institute in the city. One evening Mimiko, newly hired by the night school, was standing before his canvas. The image of her, with a garland of yellow-striped marigolds in her hair, lying on a cobalt blue satin sheet that had been spread over a settee, her full, round breasts absorbing the drops of light from the ceiling lamp, was transposed in all its living beauty to Masao's canvas.

Mimiko could hardly have survived on just her modeling job. Models at the night school worked only Mondays, Wednesdays, and Fridays.

Among the students it was rumored that she also secretly worked as a streetwalker. One of them told of having been approached by a prostitute on a dark corner in Matsuki-cho. Startled by the realization that he'd seen the woman before, modeling at the institute, the student had purchased an hour of sex with her. And, he was careful to add, it hadn't been very expensive.

The student said there was no doubt in his mind that it was the same woman who lay on the settee beneath the lamp for night classes at the art institute. He spread the story boastingly among his friends. Stressing how surprisingly cheap she had been.

One might say it was at that moment that Masao

began to feel something for her. From then on her life-force, when transferred to Masao's canvas, shimmered with the suggestion of sex; every curve and crevice of her rounded flesh exuded a hint of wild abandon.

The budlike form of her delicate body had begun to breathe in gasps like the red sobs of a sex-inflamed canna blossom. Masao discovered this sensibility for the first time in his own paintings. It shocked even him. There's been a change in my work, he thought.

None of his classmates, as they wielded their brushes, thought of themselves as painting a professional model. They were convinced that before their eyes reclined a hooker.

And in fact it was true. Modeling was a side job for Mimiko; her real career was as a prostitute, selling her sex to men. She didn't know that this had become common knowledge at the art institute. Not that there was any reason to believe she'd have stopped showing up if she had known.

Masao hadn't the money to go to the infamous Matsuki-cho and buy one of the women who gathered there. Much less could he imagine going in search of a certain hooker who also happened to be a model at his school.

In any event, the eros of the nude upon his canvas was separated from his own libido by an unthinkable, unbridgeable gulf.

As long as he lacked money, the body of the woman before his eyes was utterly out of reach. The backdrop, crimson silk embroidered with a gold lamé mesh, hung softly, weightlessly from ceiling to floor, the edge of it concealing part of the model's leg. Masao didn't know her name at the time.

He could hear his friends behind him, whispering things like:

"Loan me some money. I wanna go get a piece of this model tomorrow."

The woman's waistlength black hair was swept over one shoulder, the ends turning up and pointing outward, like stamens.

Over the round, whitewashed modeling platform had been hung a violet drop cloth of velvet; as the woman lay on the settee, the faint pink of her toenails blended gently into her flesh. Her eyes had a greenish translucence, and she blinked as if gazing at a bright, distant meadow. Her nose was straight and finely sculpted, with a provocative little upturned tip.

As he set his palette on the desk Masao looked at her, with her lissome arms angled slightly forward, guessing her age to be twenty-two or -three. There was something about the stillness in the air around her unmoving form that made it difficult to believe his talentless friend Ueno had bought this woman.

The crinkled yellow and red folds of the marigold crown on her head went well with her limpid, pool-like eyes.

The luster of her youthful skin was, by virtue of its youthfulness, a poignant sight. In this world nothing was more poignant and uncertain than the life of a woman in the prime of youth.

What remained but to age, to find as death approached that youth had been an illusion wasting away in broad daylight.

Never did the beauty of youth shine so brightly as when one learned it was just an illusion. No true understanding of youth exists in the immature minds of the young.

Masao was beginning vaguely to realize these things—ever since he'd taken up art. It was this that drove him to absorb from the model and transfer to canvas, in every detail, the life of a young woman—hair by living hair, the softness of pale pink nipples, the gentleness of graceful fingers.

It resembled that miracle of early spring: the radiance of cherry blossoms in full bloom.

Only after the frenzied scattering of blossoms did the deception become apparent: the resplendent atmosphere was changed instantaneously into one of gloom.

Youth, too, like the shock of this radical transformation, was nothing more than a mirage.

Life, as well.

Being alive was but a momentary illusion.

And after that shining illusion was gone, the eternal stillness and emptiness of death; the final destruction of this brilliant but pitiful life.

Masao was looking at the model's shadowy tangle of pubic hair, right before him. He'd never had sexual intercourse with a woman. Eros was, for him, an unexplored and mysterious wilderness. It lay buried deep in a jungle of shame and desire.

The woman before him, with her pale sex, the insinuation of libido in the very strands of her hair, spoke to him from that chasm. This vaguely sexual *objét*, enveloped in an atmosphere of gold-embroidered lamé and violet velvet, became the ghost of youth that came forward in an open appeal to the soul of the artist.

Masao's hand stiffened around the brush.

Captive to the model's every bewitching quiver and the subdued spell of Eros that commanded his soul, he felt his penis tremble and swell.

Youth's curtain soundlessly fell to bury the unfinished enchantment of the world in the silence of life; now it flaps and billows around Masao ....

The earth undulates noiselessly. Startled, Masao peers ahead to see a flower garden—foxgloves, clematises, dahlias, crocuses, pansies—rising and falling in sinuous surges. The garden stretches to the ends of the earth, and where it joins the horizon its hundred colors grow indistinct, indistinguishable, and the sun blazes even more fiercely.

The violet blue clusters of foxglove droop heavily, wilting. The tips are wrenched off to expire amid smoke and flames. Far in the distance, chrome-yellow fragments of crocus lie scorched and writhing in the sun. The eyelike centers of pansies begin to spin at tremendous speeds, the momentum causing the petals to tear free and fly into space, piercing the gaps between clouds, spraying flower juice as they scatter. Thus they disperse, dismembered.

The flowers that still remain on the ground convulse.

The entire garden writhes in anguish.

But it's not only flowers and plants. Newly matured praying mantises have their heads torn off as their green bodies copulate.

Young ants who've been busily at work are now gathered in drifts, adhering to one another like black withered seeds, festering with sticky sores as they accumulate. Even when the winds try to carry them off, the countless ant corpses cling to the earth and will not be moved.

Masao, peering again at the model, discovers a fallen column of light describing dull horizontal lines on the road through the black woods ahead, beneath a suddenly dark and cloud-heavy sky.

Those beams of light shine upon a spot below his lower abdomen and flicker in recognition. Masao reflexively drops a hand to his pubic area. Such is the extent to which all things around him have begun to evince a deep, intense connection to male sexuality.

This could scarcely occur in a life that's outlasted its usefulness.

The model remains perfectly still beneath her crown of flowers.

Standing before his partially painted canvas amid the smell of oils and turpentine and gazing into the distance beyond the model, Masao becomes aware of a faint sound, like pale red phantom thunder.

To the right he can see a great swarm of lizards with blue-white tails of light making their way slowly—so slowly they scarcely seem to breathe—from one edge of the landscape to the other.

These are the hungry-souled youngsters who come out on stage to perform between acts in the drama of life. Too young to know what to do with their youth, dripping with beauty, these beings of energy.

What is youth? Masao, whose amazement has robbed him of his voice, poses that question to the bizarre herd of lizards.

In the prime of life himself, Masao finds it all but impossible to grasp the beauty that lies even one second in the past. He's always unable to sleep at night with a canvas before him.

Perhaps in old age, when youth has long since receded into the distance, he will at last be able to breathe easy.

On sleepless nights, it's not so much the light of all the actual stars as the many-headed libido that preys on his youth and tears him apart.

Why youth? Why this springlike form? Masao, gazing at the prospect before him, shivers with the unknowable, nameless power that drives him toward life. He has no confidence in his ability to capture on canvas the beauty of human beings, of human life, of women, of love and hate.

Yet each day, on canvas, he hungers for something in the soul.

He attempts to paint it and ends up sick at heart.

Standing on trembling legs he sees this dreamlike human drama blown to pieces by a whirlwind raging in the background, behind the woman whose body gives form to Eros.

From the upper left, swarms of fireflies flit across the scene, scattering and dropping in the shadows of reeds on the surface of a river, the pale lights on the tips of their tails drawn into the water, where they're silently extinguished. Frogs hop about in the softly glowing reflection. Male and female they copulate. It's mating season for the fireflies too, who are on their way to make eggs.

A female dog with a severed tail runs through the sky. A male follows, sniffing her scent and giving chase. They begin to fuck. Their yellow, stammering yelps nearly drown out even the sound of the phantom thunder. Climbing upon a fragment of cloud, the dogs mate right there in the sky, unashamed and oblivious.

Snakes wriggle out of holes in the brush. The

females writhe suggestively atop the long, striped bodies of males.

The patterns of two entwined snakes blend together in a gradation effect until, smeared with sticky semen, they become indistinguishable, and even their outlines are lost among the shadows on the ground.

The tips of red birds' wings develop fine splits, and their feathers fall out one by one in the wind. There must be a thousand birds in the great flock, all searching for partners to mate with, joining together in midair even as they perform their endless somersaults and loops.

Iridescent semen splatters down like rain on the copulating insects that cover the ground.

Even the rumbling of phantom thunder dies out because of their screams.

Yet, amid all this uproar, the model never moves so much as an inch, standing there adrift in the floating world of lamé and velvet.

Masao peers even more closely down the path he's on, and there, lurking in the shadows of the cosmos, a clock abruptly begins to throb, beating faster even than footprints of stars several hundreds of millions of light years away, and he thinks he hears the sound of time in the world of men whisper over the cosmic stage. For a moment he wonders if it's not all just an illusion. But the drama unfolding behind the figure of the woman is far from over.

Flowers entrust their lives to the beat of the clock. At a glance, their colors seem eternal. And, yes, so it is for all things: only at first do they look eternal.

Slowly, slowly colors fade, shapes fade, to the beat of the clock.

The shadow-picture of time, faster than a falling star, enfolds all things.

And those who have life upon this stage are all drowned in the fragrance of youth, though not one of them knows it.

An intimation of ruin creeps into the background of this scene in the cosmic drama.

Sensing it, Masao lets out a gasp.

He frantically tries to capture that intimation on his canvas. But it's much too powerful for him to claim for his picture.

Life is only a momentary flash of light, and Masao believes that the power of art is eternal; yet for all his skill and concentration, it's hard to immerse himself in that overwhelming power.

Still he courageously struggles on, trying to paint it—that intimation that none of the masters of East or West has ever been able to capture.

The storm is still advancing.

Insects and snakes that the wind and rain have driven into heaps at the model's feet, and even between her toes, lie there wriggling.

The river overflows its banks, flooding the gardens.

The water knocks down reeds and laps at flower tops, soaking them.

Masao doubts his own eyes. That the cosmic drama, so beautiful only moments before, could change so quickly. Just look. One can sense a drop curtain falling between the spaces in time.

The woman, standing in the center of the stage, still shows no sign of moving, though the wind of the storm whips through her black hair.

Loaches and other fish, flushed from the river in the flood, expose their white scales to the sky and gasp for breath as they flop about in agony on the velvet drop cloth where the woman stands.

More loaches adhere, flapping, to the lamé, with its embroidered brocade.

Hundreds of them are stuck flat to the multi-colored, glistening material. Male and female, all of them dying in the act of copulation.

Baby fish, with their undeveloped sex organs concealed beneath tail fins, are breathing their last. Working their immature gills, they leave their many lives lying there, like the last rays of a setting sun.

The frogs are pregnant.

If the drastic transformation of the stage had come a bit later, perhaps youth would have advanced one more step. But after the changes brought by time to the cosmic drama, all living beings grow old and enfeebled, lose their beauty and charm, and turn to skeletons in the midst of desolation.

Masao can scarcely believe that even in this aging landscape, the goddess of beauty, Aphrodite, maintains her youth forever.

To him it's clearly a miracle that amid the degeneration of youthfulness, this woman alone manages to keep time at a standstill.

Peer as he might, he can see not even the slightest hint that the woman's young body will ever grow old. This tranquil organic being will stand forever in the torn canvas within the frame where time has stopped.

Masao doubts his eyes, wondering if it isn't some glitch in his grasp of reality. But reality is unfolding before him. This must be a cold dream frozen fast in the cosmos.

One mysterious corner of this superreality is a space one might call maniacally graphic.

It even seems to Masao as if the shadows of the model's breasts and pubic hair, amid the uncanny rumbling of the phantom thunder of heaven, have pinioned the earth for a moment with the rigidity of lust.

What shape does the beauty of this woman's life take?

He focuses his gaze ahead.

In that instant, his brush, canvas, paints—all vanish.

The brush falls from his dumbfounded hand.

Behold: the golden frame around her blends into the enchanted air and vanishes without a trace.

It's at this moment that Masao unmistakably hears, beating upon his eardrums, the footsteps of phantasmal existence retreating into the background of life.

Not even art can stop it; behind art is the bottomless space of the cosmos, moving with each moment. Art and the earth, and human beings, are all in the process of being destroyed. All in the process of becoming extinct.

All living beings are passing away.

As Masao marvels at what lies in the background of life, the storm grows in power, and the scenery behind the model is laid to waste by the wind.

Living creatures one and all are leaving their corpses scattered upon the ground.

Like drifting snow, carcasses of the young pile high in a circle around the woman and at her feet, preparing to greet the darkness of night.

With day lingering over this map of hell and the storm having passed, the afterglow of stars shines through a fissure in the cloudy sky and focuses upon that putrid smell.

The woman is still standing there.

Masao, having lost all the instruments of his art—frame, brush, paints—approaches the woman with the antennae of his heart.

He reaches out his hand to her firm, white skin. But when he touches her full and shapely breast, the woman's body crumbles and collapses, bestrewing the area with the clattering sound of nothingness.

Her body was made of lime; now that she's fallen apart a white cloud of dust rises toward heaven, grazing the starlight.

Looking down at the ground, he can see that all the corpses of youth, in their ruined states, are turning to stone.

Transformed into an infinite number of pebbles.

The woman's eye, a fragment of limestone, lies among them, gazing at a fixed point on the horizon.

One of her arms has broken off and is caught on the dorsal fin of a fossilized fish.

The region of her once dense, black pubic hair has been pulverized; not a trace remains. The interval of Eros has become a black ruin that wafts about in the air.

Hollow Eros expanding to fill the empty space.

Just as with bridge girders reflected in a river, the real image and the ghost image join to form an illusory circle; an Eros that is merely there, with no purpose.

Where did that shape go? That fresh and comely, voluptuous form?

The beauty and Eros that Masao felt just moments

ago, with all his sensibilities and all his reason, to be his—where have they gone?

He searches the area in a frenzy, as if deranged.

But they have hidden themselves beyond the bubbles of transience.

O days of lovely earthly illusion!

The flower garden of youth we once pursued—where is it now?

In spite of all the tools of art we believed were in our grasp, the beauty and pale green Eros of youth have collapsed into rubbish, wasted.

Nothingness pummels Masao's entire body. Captive to his own despair.

One point of light shines upon the ground. Masao sees the glow of a delicate little rainbow that's alighted there.

Wondering, he reaches out to pluck it between his fingers, and retrieves a single splash of lamé.

Separated from the gold-embroidered drop cloth that hangs from the ceiling, it has just fluttered down to the floor.

Masao brings the drop of lamé closer to the pupils of his eyes. It sparkles in the glow of the ceiling lamps. And amid those angular, shimmering lights he returned to his senses.

He rose to his feet when the instructor signaled the end of the modeling session.

The model came out of her pose and began putting on her dress right in front of him.

The evening's lesson was over. Masao studied the canvas beside him, then took it in his hands and ripped it apart.

For all the passion he'd put into sketching the

model, she'd become nothing more than a soulless ghost on the canvas.

The sketch didn't satisfy even a smidgen of his heart's quest for beauty. To capture beauty was a thing of tremendous difficulty, yes, but the thought did nothing to appease his heart.

Without thinking, he broke his paint brush in two. In the rear courtyard of the institute he doused the canvas with thinner and set it on fire.

In no time at all red tongues of flame were licking at various parts of the woman's body—her breasts, her pubic hair ... The garland of marigolds, too, was disappearing in fire.

Masao stood before the burning canvas, his soul drawn to the woman departing with the flames into darkness.

In one corner of his abstracted mind he became aware of someone nearby.

It almost seemed as if the woman were speaking to him from amid the blaze. An illusion of some sort, he thought. Startled, he peered more closely into the fire, and the model's face rose up in the flames.

Beyond the flames was darkness.

She spoke to him from the blazing canvas.

"My portrait! Why did you burn it?"

Gazing bewildered at his face.

"Because, no matter how hard I try to capture beauty," he said, "it always eludes me."

"I have one of your drawings," the woman surprised him by saying. "You threw it away, and I picked it up off the floor and framed it."

She stepped around the fire and approached him.

She was smaller than he'd thought, so much so

that it was hard to believe she was the same woman who'd stood on the modeling platform. She scarcely came up to his shoulders.

"What's your name?" he asked her.

"Mimiko," she said, staring off into the darkness beyond the flames. "I'd like to show you the drawing I have of yours."

She said she lived up the narrow lane behind the institute, on the side of the hill known as Shiroyama.

They set off together up the dark little path, trampling the dew on the summer grass.

The sky descended above them, bearing a faint scent of flowers. The white fragrance enveloped Masao's body.

When he looked ahead, he saw that the acacia-lined path continued up the hill, the pale white clusters of flowers filling the gaps in the star-studded sky, spreading overhead like a white dome that defied the highlands darkness.

Turning to look back, he could see the lights of houses in town sparkling between the black trunks of acacia trees, like rubies embedded in a dark wooden sculpture. The points of light pierced his pupils.

As the red gemlike lights were scattered and lost behind them, his brain grew all the more disordered.

He could scarcely believe that the woman he'd studied so many times on the modeling platform was now walking along beside him. Mimiko, she said her name was. He murmured the name in his heart, suddenly filled with curiosity. What sort of life did this woman lead? It made his pulse quicken to think that soon he would get a glimpse of her world.

The house stood at the end of the dark tunnel of

acacia trees. It was little more than a run-down shack. The glass of the sliding front door was broken in several places, but this was scarcely the sort of house one would bother to lock. Inside, it was even shabbier than the cheap apartment Masao had been staying in—there wasn't a single piece of proper furniture. Splintered mikan crates that sat directly upon the tatami mats, loosely covered with a tattered old madder-red piece of vinyl, served as a makeshift table. The teacups upon it looked as if they hadn't been washed for days, and when the woman switched on the bare bulb hanging from the ceiling, they reflected the light with a solitary, somber glow.

There was only one room. Stepping up into it from the concrete entryway, Masao glanced at the far corner, and his heart stopped. Crouched there was what appeared to be a squirming human form.

This form turned to face him with a quick, nervous movement like that of a wild bird. Sensing Masao's astonishment, Mimiko quickly explained.

"That's my little brother. I take care of him. He likes toy trains. Sometimes I buy them for him in town."

As if to confirm her words, the boy, of indeterminate age, who was sitting with rounded shoulders that gave him the appearance of a hunchback, his pallid face drooping over the floor, now picked up with paralyzed hands a toy locomotive in front of him and held it out silently toward Masao. Masao just looked at him, at a loss as to how to respond, and the little brother, dripping a steady stream of drool down the front of his striped shirt, opened his mouth slightly and shouted an unintelligible "Ahh! Ahh!" There was no telling what he wanted. The toy locomotive must have been too heavy for him and soon fell from his hands. It hit the floor with a clatter and landed upside-down, its wheels spinning around and around. Apparently, whenever Mimiko was out working, this boy sat home alone in the darkness—for surely he wouldn't be capable of switching on the light by himself—and forlornly awaited her return.

Mimiko told Masao her mother had died some years before, of a stroke; long before that, her father had vanished to places unknown. She'd obviously had no choice but to assume the care of her brother.

Masao was nonplused; he was having difficulty reconciling the woman sitting before him in this wretched, run-down little shack of a house with the model who'd stood against that glittering backdrop of lamé and velvet.

But he'd already known that she made a living as a prostitute in the streets of Matsuki-cho. As he remembered this, emotion welled up in his breast. It was hardly inconceivable that a woman who sold her body to support an incurably disabled brother would be forced to live in such squalor. She's poor, that's all, he thought, looking vacantly up at the soot-covered ceiling as he sat down on the tatami and breathed a deep but silent sigh.

Masao himself was far from well off: he couldn't even buy all the paint he needed. But at least he didn't have any relatives dependent on him.

He couldn't afford his own apartment and saved rent by staying with his friend, another art student.

He was reflecting upon the circumstances of his own life and toying with the tip of a spoon he'd picked up from the floor when he noticed his sketch hanging in a primitive frame on the wall above Mimiko's disabled brother, who sat there shaking his head meaninglessly.

"That's the portrait you were talking about, is it?" he said. "I threw that away because it's not any good. Next time I'll do a real portrait of you, in oil paints, as a present."

Mimiko smoothed out the hem of her dark gray-checked dress and smiled with innocent, childlike delight.

That was how the two of them had met.

The trees of the acacia grove hung thickly above the roof of the house, and at this time each year the blossoms continued to fall and scatter silently over these grounds.

Three years had passed since that first season of falling flowers in which they'd met and fallen in love, and after which they'd begun to live together in this house. The only major changes in that time were that Mimiko, having become Masao's wife, had no longer needed to walk the streets of Matsuki-cho selling her body, and that her disabled brother had died suddenly of pneumonia one cold winter day. She'd buried his body on the snow-covered hill behind the house, next to their mother's grave. Early each summer the acacias still bloomed in profusion and fell in a steady stream over the roof of the house.

But the small life-space that Masao had happened upon with his penniless prostitute hadn't lasted for long.

Cancer had begun to attack Mimiko's body. It started in the spot most vital to a woman—the uterus.

Mimiko grew thinner and more emaciated with each passing day. The cancer spread throughout her body, eating away at her once beautiful flesh, violating her completely, and finally robbing her of life. Every night since then he'd slept with her remains, drying the corpse in the garden sunlight each afternoon.

In this loathsome season of love, acacia season, both you and I are bedecked with flowers, but between us we have no feathered robe with which to take wing and fly.

The only gift of this short and insignificant season of flesh and blood: an instant of whiteness at dawn.

Was it a wound we don't want to recall, asleep in the depths of the sea? Or the loss of a moment as brief as a kiss?

Once again the time of acacia blossoms has come. Sex aches with a cold, sharp pain, in a frozen season unentangled with living love; look up at the treetops: the air grows tense with a sigh.

A dream that appeared in the season of falling flowers. Fanciful copulation with a corpse is the ultimate emptiness: thus ends young love, and lost memories are but signal fires proclaiming the passion we've missed in the days of hallucination.

Was he just hearing things? The voices of a young couple flirting.

Human hearts, wandering forlorn paths between the trees.

Closing his eyes and listening, he could hear the beat of the clock as it flowed away in an instant, tears accumulating, becoming a brook, the brook becoming a stream, the stream flowing into a great river, the soul pouring into the harbor of sorrow, the vast expanse of sea in the distance, and while love pretends to forgive, it seems to embrace our most desperate prayers.

And, ah, once again the acacia season arrives on earth. Only despair has deepened, solitude that quivers like the white asshole of a rabbit, genitals washed periodically with the dripping juice of wild strawberries. Since the day we flew off on wounded wings, the weight of a hundred million light years.

Already late for the season, the soul in its lonely hole. The emptiness embodied by the postmortem sex of this man and woman. When love is buried in flowers, the soul becomes ugly, dulled like the pearl on a ring, until even the adored figure itself is lost from view. O infant, born somewhere on earth this morning: What color the mold that forms your flesh? And yet, who knows? This season of regret. O death smell acacia!

Masao removed the mirror from Mimiko's dressing table. He wanted to find her inside it.

But she was nowhere to be seen on the cold, icy surface of the mirror. Not even a rear view of gorgeous youth, whisked off across rippling fields of wheat in the warm summer wind. Still he searched for her plump young cheeks, but not even lips to kiss could he find.

"Mimiko!" he cried, pursuing the hint of an image.

And what appeared now was the haggard, hollow-cheeked face of a wretched man.

Overnight his hair had grown whiter than snow. His eyes were sunken inside their sockets. The face was streaked with tears of hopelessness. A face that hadn't been washed for a week.

The beard had been left to grow, and his chin was hidden beneath the tangles. The face was wrinkled, old.

Masao was startled to find himself there, wounded in the midst of a youth that had fled so abruptly.

He could not deny that this mirrored self was the aged figure he'd always been destined to be.

To continue to look at that image was more than his aching heart could bear.

With all his strength he smashed the mirror against the concrete of the entryway, sending a spray of mote-sized diamonds scattering in every direction. Standing there among them he glanced out at the garden, and the shock he received sent him dashing outside.

Looking about, he saw that all things had been obliterated, reduced to a haze of nothingness.

Like a madman he scratched with his hands at the ground where Mimiko's corpse had been, searching for her.

Her body had decomposed, eaten by maggots, the rotting meat dried to powder, a speck of matter in the universe, returned now to the soil of the earth.

All that remained were the acacia petals strewn over the ground and the swarms of insects digesting her rotted flesh. Overlapping, one upon the other, they multiplied endlessly. Accumulating until they reached the horizon and beyond.

A suddenly cloudy corner of sky sent an interval swollen with wind to the earth.

The wind had come from the ends of the universe to rustle the leaves of the acacia forest, and an enormous cloud of white pollen rose to envelop the treetops.

Flower petals drew dizzying spirals as they danced up into the sky, fell back to earth, then ascended once again to dye the entire universe silver-gray.

The lives of corollas, heaped high and full in the sun, swept away with the wind in the wink of an eye.

O wind, I beg you, cease your raging. Do not destroy them. The lives of these flowers, already so brief. Refrain from destroying the forest of youth ....

Futility came with the wind.

The wind scattered its phantom flowers upon the earth, one petal after another, tirelessly.

Afterwards only the forest treetops, regressed to skeletal nothingness, scattering bleached leaf-veins and patterns of flowers, pollen, calyces, stamens, pistils.

The distance between heaven and earth returns to nothing, and all that remains adrift in that space is the lonely hush of an empty heart.

Afterword

Imagine discovering that Joseph Cornell, Andy Warhol or Eva Hesse were prolific writers of fiction and poetry. Yayoi Kusama—the celebrated modern master of radical art—has been discovered. Like her painting and collages, sculpture, environments and Happenings that are now icons of the 1960s, her writing is hallucinatory, structured by repetition, and obsessed with sexual imagery that is violent, fantastic and laughable all at once. Kusama's madness is legendary, but mental illness is not artistry and its debris is not art: Her novels and poetry have acquired cult status in Japan's literary vanguard since *Manhattan Suicide Addict*, her autobiographical novel of life as an artist in downtown New York, was first published in 1978. If her vast artistic production represents a ferocious struggle to master the images that revolt or terrify her by repeatedly recreating them under her aesthetic control, then her fiction, which until recently has not been available in English translation, offers further evidence of Kusama's extraordinary powers to transform the chimerical illusions of the mind into enduring art.

Since Kusama first emerged as a self-described "independent" in Tokyo's contemporary art

Afterword

establishment in the early 1950s, she has claimed in numerous interviews and statements that her work "is related to my internal problems." Later in her 1975 manifesto, "Struggles and Wanderings of My Soul," Kusama describes a life of mental battle against recurring hallucinations that include visions of ghastly multiplication and fragmentation, sensations of being separated from reality behind a vast veil of nets, and her self-obliteration by forces of infinite voidness. It was such phantasmic hallucinations that "drove me to paint," Kusama writes, and generated what she later identified as her unique practice of "obsessional art." Simultaneously, recurring visions obsessed her and she was obsessed by giving them form, as if the compulsive act to create would triumph over the terror that repeatedly threatened to dissolve her being. Kusama's path of obsessional art has saved her, she suggests, from total despair and probable suicide; it has also certified her originality *vis à vis* the dominant contemporary art fashions which she disdains utterly. Diagnosed as a young woman with an obsessive-compulsive and hysteric condition, she has since 1977 been a voluntary resident in a psychiatric institution in Tokyo. It is there that she has turned to writing as an alternative form of artistic expression and therapeutic practice. Writing through the nights in her asylum cubicle, she has produced thirteen books in Japanese including novels, poetry anthologies and compilations of short stories.

This volume presents three of Kusama's most well-known novellas superbly translated by Ralph F. McCarthy. Their themes that center so intensely on castration fantasy, hallucination, and suicidal ideation are familiar to us from Kusama's own life yet she denies that they are autobiographical. "It goes without saying that one needs imagination to write a work of literature....Shimako, the protagonist of *Foxgloves of Central Park*, is of course the product of imagination: Shimako is not me." Set in New York or Japan in the present time, they recount the adventures of a cast of multiethnic characters living at the fringes of society. Their destitute yet spectacular lives revolve around drug addiction and psychiatric illness, incest, rape and prostitution, orphanhood, loss of a beloved and suicide. The renowned novelist Ryu Murakami has remarked that Kusama's stories that reel from the sordid to carnivalesque are reminiscent of Jean Genet's fictions of depraved city underworlds in the sense that "both make filth shine." But unlike Genet, Kusama's rhapsodic melodramas embrace the surreal and remain fixed in another world where "spirits wander between reality and image."

In 1983, *The Hustlers Grotto on Christopher Street* won Japan's prestigious Literary Award for New Writers given by the monthly magazine *Yasei jidai*. The jury consisted of the notable novelists Masahiro Mita, Michitsuna Takahashi, Teru Miyamoto, Ryu Murakami and Kenji Nakagami. This group, a generation or two younger than the postwar school of Japanese literature advanced by such giants as Kōbō Abe, Yukio Mishima and Kenzaburō Ōe, had emerged as the leaders of a new genre of contemporary Japanese fiction. As intellectual nihilists who came of age in the 1960s, they eschewed Abe's existentialism, Mishima's romanticism, and Ōe's political ideology for a more fantastic, even psychedelic style of fiction. Their tales of bizarre violence, erotic obsessions and occult happenings—a kind of postmodern magic

Afterword

realism—were inspired in part by their revival of an eccentric strain in early modern Japanese literature identified by the writings of Izumi Kyōka (1873-1939). Viewed as peripheral during his lifetime because he stood independent of the dominant modern trend of literary naturalism, Kyōka had invoked folklore, superstition and legend to create a fictive purgatory of the supernatural and grotesque. What appealed to avant-garde writers of the 1970s and eighties was his graphic imagery, gothic decadence and dark premodern sensibility. It is not surprising that Kusama, who ranks Kyōka topmost among her favorite Japanese writers, emerged in Tokyo's literary world at the height of the "Kyōka boom" and later established close association with three of her jurors—Miyamoto, Murakami, and Nakagami—who today are internationally recognized for ushering in the "new Japanese fiction." Like these novelists, Kusama writes about a macabre, supernatural world haunted with strange forms of love and betrayal in a language that is equally visual, formalist and stylized. Nakagami especially admired Kusama's commitment to exploring the taboo territories of violence, discrimination, incest and bisexuality—a terrain he knew well. The risks Kusama's fiction takes with its pictorial prose and open ambiguities between "this world" and the world of apparitions can hence best be tolerated by positioning her work in Kyōka's supernaturalist lineage.

Kusama's literary style can also be attributed to her lifelong association with Surrealism. Surrealism's essential preoccupation with the processes of the unconscious mind, its practice of automatism, and its dedication to what Paul Klee called the "instinct which drives us downward, deep down to the primal source" have consistently provided a critical framework for the appreciation of Kusama's visual art, from her early biomorphic watercolors to her later psychosexual sculptures. Surrealism, which artists employed in prewar Japan as a veiled critique of the totalitarian state, also created for Kusama her identification with the humanist left-wing for whom fantasy (*gensō*) was encoded with social critique and political subversion. Through constructing a world of poetic illusion, art could offer an escape from the mechanistic oppression of a dominant state apparatus and modern bourgeois society. Kusama's outrage against authoritarianism was informed by this radical avant-garde stance and has imparted the urgency of social concern to works like her *Driving Image* series and antiwar Happenings of the 1960s. In her fiction as well, Kusama constructs fantasy (hallucinations from drugs or madness) in opposition to outside systems of phallocentric authority, which she depicts in a myriad of versions as traumatic and abusive.

Kusama's characters—most obviously Henry in *The Hustlers Grotto on Christopher Street*—are Pop-like reductions, stereotypical caricatures of the African American male, the junkie, the homosexual hustler. Like all her subjects both animate and inanimate, her characters are highly eroticized and therefore not "realistic;" like all Pop artists, she forgoes realism in favor of stylization. She is less concerned with drawing out her characters than using them as conduits of an excessive phantasmagoria. Kusama is also delivering her subversive critique of New York's chauvinist art world where women and outsiders are forced to survive, like Henry, as exotic

Afterword

objects of power and sexual abuse. Social relations in Kusama's world inevitably produce the "curtain of depersonalization" that separates the self from others and renders mundane reality into nothing but a "silvery void." To Kusama, Henry's fate is symptomatic and metaphoric of a rottenness at society's core and yet here, she finds her voice as an artist.

The fright, anxiety and panic that rule Kusama's characters and give such frenzy to her narratives arise by some creative genealogy from her own traumatic experiences that have psychically obsessed her for some fifty years. Daniel Paul Schreber, the famous Wilhelmine-era psychotic whose asylum notebooks describing visions of being sodomized by the "rays" of God provided Freud some of his most important material for analyzing paranoia, remains current because of what others extrapolate from his illness. Kusama, a mental patient like Schreber, herself extrapolates from her illness; again and again she triumphs over her trauma by shaping it into art. While imaginary forces continue to transgress and disrupt her notions of phenomenal realism, confirming her status as an outsider, she emerges through her art and writing as the consummate insider. As readers, we too stride that edge.

—*Alexandra Munroe, Fall 1997*

Yayoi Kusama, born in 1929 in Japan, is an internationally recognized artist. From 1958 to 1973 she lived and worked in New York City and since 1977, has been a voluntary resident in a psychiatric hospital in Tokyo. She has exhibited widely in Europe, America and Asia including museum retrospective exhibitions at the Center for International Arts, New York in 1989 and the Japanese Pavilion of the Venice Biennial in 1993. From 1998-99, a touring survey of her work organized by the Los Angeles County Museum of Art and the Museum of Modern Art, New York travels to the Walker Art Center in Minneapolis and the Museum of Contemporary Art, Tokyo. A poet and novelist, she has published thirteen books since 1978 that have earned her cult status in Japan's literary vanguard. In 1983, she was awarded Japan's prestigious Literary Award for New Writers given by the monthly magazine* Yasei jidai.

Ralph F. McCarthy is a writer, translator, and lyricist who lives in Los Angeles and Tokyo. His previous translations include books by Osamu Dazai and Ryu Murakami.

Alexandra Munroe is an independent curator based in New York and Tokyo, and MacCracken Fellow of East Asian Studies at New York University. A leading authority on modern Japanese art, she is author of Yayoi Kusama: A Retrospective (1989) *and* Japanese Art After 1945: Scream Against the Sky (1994).